FROM OUT OF THE DARKNESS

came the sound of evil laughter, louder and louder, until I thought I would go mad with fear. And then I saw him—the face, pale and punched with shadow, but with the long nose, the shoulder-length hair and forked beard, unmistakably the Black Baron himself, who had been dead for at least five hundred years!

As he reached for the ladder, I choked back a startled sob and began to run. I reached the steps and was scrambling up them as fast as I could when I felt iron fingers digging cruelly into my shoulder, wrenching me back sharply. Then I was falling, flying through the air until something struck the back of my head. **There was a loud clanging sound which quickly faded, and then everything went black. . . .**

More SIGNET Gothics by Caroline Farr

- [ ] **ROOM OF SECRETS** (#E8965—$1.75)*
- [ ] **DARK CITADEL** (#Y7552—$1.25)
- [ ] **ISLAND OF EVIL** (#W8476—$1.50)*
- [ ] **HEIRESS OF FEAR** (#W8300—$1.50)*
- [ ] **SINISTER HOUSE** (#W7892—$1.50)
- [ ] **CASTLE ON THE RHINE** (#W8615—$1.50)*
- [ ] **SIGNET DOUBLE GOTHIC—WITCHES' HAMMER and GRANITE FOLLY** (#J8360—$1.95)*
- [ ] **SIGNET DOUBLE GOTHIC—HOUSE OF DARK ILLUSION and THE SECRET OF THE CHATEAU** (#E7662—$1.75)
- [ ] **CASTLE ON THE LOCH** (#E8830—$1.75)*
- [ ] **CASTLE OF TERROR** (#E8900—$1.75)*

* Price slightly higher in Canada

Buy them at your local bookstore or use this convenient coupon for ordering.

THE NEW AMERICAN LIBRARY, INC.,
P.O. Box 999, Bergenfield, New Jersey 07621

Please send me the SIGNET BOOKS I have checked above. I am enclosing $_____(please add 50¢ to this order to cover postage and handling). Send check or money order—no cash or C.O.D.'s. Prices and numbers are subject to change without notice.

Name _____

Address _____

City_____ State_____ Zip Code_____

Allow 4-6 weeks for delivery.
This offer is subject to withdrawal without notice.

Secret at Ravenswood

By
Caroline Farr

A SIGNET BOOK
NEW AMERICAN LIBRARY
TIMES MIRROR
in association with Horwitz Publications

NAL BOOKS ARE AVAILABLE AT QUANTITY DISCOUNTS
WHEN USED TO PROMOTE PRODUCTS OR SERVICES. FOR
INFORMATION PLEASE WRITE TO PREMIUM MARKETING
DIVISION, THE NEW AMERICAN LIBRARY, INC., 1633
BROADWAY, NEW YORK, NEW YORK 10019.

COPYRIGHT © 1980 BY HORWITZ PUBLICATIONS, A DIVISION OF
HORWITZ GROUP BOOKS PTY LTD. (HONG KONG BRANCH), HONG
KONG B.C.C.

Reproduction in part or in whole in any language expressly forbidden in any part of the world without the written consent of Horwitz Publications.

All rights reserved. For information address Horwitz Cammeray Centre, 506 Miller Street, P.O. Box 306, Cammeray 2062, Australia.

SIGNET TRADEMARK REG. U.S. PAT. OFF. AND FOREIGN COUNTRIES
REGISTERED TRADEMARK—MARCA REGISTRADA
HECHO EN CHICAGO, U.S.A.

SIGNET, SIGNET CLASSICS, MENTOR, PLUME, MERIDIAN AND NAL
BOOKS *are published by The New American Library, Inc.,
1633 Broadway, New York, New York 10019*

FIRST PRINTING, APRIL, 1980

1 2 3 4 5 6 7 8 9

PRINTED IN THE UNITED STATES OF AMERICA

Secret at Ravenswood

1

James Montague formed his long bony fingers into a spire and asked me how I was enjoying London. I told him just fine; there were so many things to see and do, and the one thing I lacked was time.

"Yes, I daresay," he said with a smile. "It's a far cry from Chicago. Shropshire is even more so. It's quite beautiful up there, even wild in parts. You'll like it, I'm sure."

"I don't know if I'll have time to see much of it," I pointed out. "I will be rather busy. So much cataloging to do. Such an enormous library."

He chuckled good-humoredly. "There you are. You Americans. Such a preoccupation with time." Still with his fingers pressed together, he swiveled his chair from side to side and beamed at me. "It's all go, isn't it? Oh, well. Yes, let's see." He stopped moving, lowered his hands, and looked down at some papers on the desk in front of him. "The arrangements have all been made. All that remains is getting you to Ravenswood. I suppose you'll be wanting to go as soon as possible."

"As soon as possible," I agreed. "There's nothing to keep me in London. And the collection has to be back in Chicago by the end of the month, so, you see, there isn't really very much time."

He looked up from the papers. "You're very young," he remarked equably. "I had expected someone so much older. . . ." He spread his hands, turning them palms upward. "Well, a librarian. One has preconceptions of librarians as fusty, severe, wearing thick glasses, and crisply efficient. I was wrong, wasn't I?"

His smile was infectious, and I found myself smiling back at him. "You make it sound as if you were expecting a dragon."

"Perhaps I was. Well, someone very bookish certainly. I was quite prepared to feel intimidated. You don't make me feel intimidated at all."

"But I really am quite efficient," I told him.

"Oh, I'm sure you must be," he said quickly. "Otherwise you would hardly be handling the Watmough Collection."

If he had had any preconceptions about me as a librarian, I was sure that my own preconceptions about him had been given just as much of a jolt some minutes before, when he had come out of his office, greeted me, and ushered me into the room ahead of him.

I guess I had been expecting something . . . well, a little more orderly. Somewhere at the back of my mind, perhaps, I thought there was no reason why a London solicitor's offices should have been so vastly different from how I had seen them depicted in movies, or imagined them from descriptions in books. If I had really thought about it at all, I suppose I would have pictured James Montague's office as being nicely carpeted and book-lined, with comfortable leather armchairs and a fire flickering cheerfully in an open fireplace. Tea—Earl Grey, possibly—would be served from a silver pot. The china would be delicate but durable, brought in on a silver tray by one of those brisk, sturdy people who always crop up in English movies—spinsterish and devoted, yet not prepared to put up with any nonsense. The windows would look over a park, the river, or perhaps St. Paul's Cathedral, and the atmosphere would be understated, quietly traditional.

There was one window in James Montague's office, but the only view it afforded was of a pocked stone wall and a portion of fire escape. And far from being spacious and comfortable, there was barely room in the office for the two of us, the desk, the two straight-backed chairs, and the shelves that were packed full of books, piles of folders, and rolled-up legal briefs tied with mauve ribbon. The battered, scarred desk was cluttered with more books, folders, briefs, and papers, all of which were sprinkled with pipe tobacco and marked with overlapping brown rings where he had placed his teacup down on them. The telephone stood on the windowsill behind the desk, along with two empty teacups, a pipe rack with two pipes, a round tin of pipe tobacco, and a desk calendar that had been scribbled over extensively. A small electric heater stood against one wall, next to a gray metal filing cabinet. The room was warm and stuffy, and redolent of stale pipe tobacco.

The tea he had brought in himself, shouldering his way through the half-open door with two china mugs filled to the brim and a plate of biscuits and slices of pink and yellow cake with pale yellow icing. "Tea's up," he announced cheerfully, putting the plate down on top of some papers on the desk and handing me one of the mugs. His own, I had noticed, was chipped. Tea had slopped over the sides of both mugs. "Biscuits and Battenberg. Help yourself." He had moved back around behind the desk to his chair. "I hope I've put in enough sugar."

Earlier I had told him I didn't take sugar, but I let it go. The tea was awfully sweet.

Now he was leaning forward across the crowded desk again. "It's all set, then," he said, his gray eyes resting lightly on mine. "I've arranged to run you up to Ravenswood tomorrow and introduce you to Lady Watmough—and speaking of dragons . . ." Swiveling his chair, he picked one of the pipes from the rack on the windowsill behind him, then took up the round tobacco tin. He opened the tin, and while I waited for him to continue, he began to pack the coarse black tobacco into the pipe, pressing it down with his thumb. He seemed to have all the time in the world at his disposal. "Smooth the passage, as it were," he said at last, looking up at me again. "Hand you over. The old girl is something of an eccentric, and frankly, I don't know how you're going to take to her." The pipe bowl was full, and he gave the tobacco one last press with his thumb. Then he held the pipe as if undecided what to do with it. "Anyway, it's all part of the service." He nodded to the plate of biscuits and cake. "Do have some Battenberg."

The cake was quite nice. The icing was marzipan. I took another sip of thick, sweet tea and tried not to grimace. Placing the filled pipe down beside him, he began to shuffle through some papers on the desk.

"Now, Miss Baker . . ." He looked up again. "Do I have to keep calling you Miss Baker? Miss what Baker?"

"Ali," I told him.

"As in Baba? Or MacGraw?"

"I guess . . . I don't know. It's really Alicia, but I've never liked it much. I was named after a great-aunt who was quite rich."

"Yes, it does sound rather like starch and lavender water. Do you mind then if I call you Ali? 'Miss Baker' sounds much too formal."

"No, I don't mind."

"And I'm James. What happened to your great-aunt? Did you come into a fortune?"

"No. She left it all to a home for abandoned pets. She loved animals."

"More tea?"

"No, thanks."

He had one of those pleasant, easygoing personalities that appealed to me. It had struck me from the moment he had come bounding into the outer office, where he had bumped against the desk at which a buxom, heavily peroxided receptionist was idly leafing through a magazine; kicked over a wastepaper basket; then, introducing himself, had ushered me into his small, dusty, overcrowded office.

He was much younger than I had expected, in his mid-twenties, perhaps a year or two older than I was, and he gave an impression of breathless, boyish enthusiasm. Even if he hadn't knocked against the desk and kicked over the wastepaper basket, apologizing profusely to the receptionist, who had glared coldly back at him, I would have suspected him to be a clumsy person. His untidiness was manifest. I liked him.

He was tall and rangy, and altogether bony, yet there was something strikingly attractive about him. He had a very expressive face. His gray eyes, deep-set above high cheekbones, held a suggestion of wry amusement, and his smile was perfectly disarming. He had a cleft chin and a longish nose. His thick dark hair was slightly but enhancingly disheveled. He was wearing a crumpled dark gray three-piece suit and a blue-and-white-striped shirt, the top button of which was laid bare by the askew plain maroon tie.

"Now that all the heavy work has been done," he said, "all that remains falls into the category of liaison work. That's my pigeon. The big guns have roared, and now there's nothing much left to do except for you to carry out your inventory and arrange to have the collection shipped back to Chicago. The shouting and the tumult die, masses of correspondence and transatlantic telephone calls, and now here we are, after all the exchanges, getting down to the final details . . . and so, another priceless heritage leaves our shores."

"That's not fair!" I retorted, stung by the ease with which he had made the comment. "When you consider it, that's not fair at all. Priceless, yes—but heritage? The collection belongs to everyone. Sir Charles Watmough must have realized that when he bequeathed it to the Institute. I mean, if it is really part of *anybody's* heritage—and I'm talking about the manuscripts—it must be those countries from which he took them in the first place. They are the ones who can honestly be said to have a prior and justifiable claim." I could feel the heat suffusing my face. Sitting upright, I shifted my position on the hard, uncomfortable chair. "To say it is a *British* heritage, I think, is . . . well, a little smug."

There was a brightness in his eyes as he watched me. His lips were curved in a half-smile. "I was really joking," he said quietly, "but I see I've managed to touch a raw nerve. Sorry about that. It's one of my more unfortunate traits. I seem to have the knack of rubbing people the wrong way." The smile faded. "No, seriously, I'm with you all the way." He laughed softly. "Let's face it, most of this so-called heritage is based on plunder. The storehouses of the world ransacked, the booty

SECRET AT RAVENSWOOD

brought back and established with such an air of piety, eyes heavenward, to the greater glory of God and Empire—and there's no doubt that Sir Charles, God rest his soul, was just as great a pirate as any of the robber barons whose descendants are now the cherished cream of society. The greater the crime, the greater the respectability. Perhaps, in a way, it's fitting that the collection is now going to find a permanent home in Chicago."

"Why's that?" I asked.

"I don't know. For some reason the image of Al Capone just passed fleetingly through my mind." He shrugged. "Now, where were we? Yes, getting you up to Ravenswood. As I said, it's part of the service, as the trustee of the estate. And I myself being a very junior partner indeed, I am only too willing to place myself at your disposal." He rummaged among the papers on the desk and found a ball-point pen. "So if you tell me where you're staying I'll pick you up in the morning. Around nine, okay?"

I was staying at a small private hotel in South Kensington. I told him the address, and that nine would be okay. He scribbled the address on a memo pad, and tearing off the sheet, folded it and tucked it into the pocket of his vest.

"Fine," he said, swinging his chair away from the desk so abruptly that his arm dislodged a sheaf of papers and sent them sliding over the edge of the desk onto the floor. Ignoring them, he stood up. "That's all arranged, then. I'll pick you up in the morning."

Pushing back my chair, I rose to my feet. "I do appreciate your help."

"Not at all. Anything for a diversion from dry and dusty corporate wrangles." He looked at me closely. "You're very pretty, if you don't mind my saying so. Blue eyes and fair hair. Surely a fine English rose."

I felt myself blushing, and averted my eyes.

"And you didn't finish your tea," he said in a tone of mild reproach.

2

To say that the Watmough behest came as a complete surprise to the Barthelmy Institute would be an exaggeration, yet it did represent a considerable windfall. The collection of books and manuscripts, one of the finest of its kind dealing with the history, religion, and culture of the Middle East, was the result of a lifetime's assiduous gleaning by the noted English Orientalist and diplomat Sir Charles Watmough, whose death some two years earlier had prompted a two-column obituary in the London *Times*.

The Barthelmy Institute for Middle Eastern Studies was a privately endowed foundation set up for the purpose, it was stated, of promoting understanding of that part of the world, but it had since grown into a multifaceted organization whose activities, I suspected, were not quite so clear-cut. There were political and economic overtones, and a sort of hushed aura that characterized the comings and goings. As the assistant librarian, I was aware of certain tremors, particularly at times of crisis, and could associate them with the references that were being demanded from the library.

The Institute was tightly compartmented. We all worked in, as it were, sealed chambers. The green demand slips came down the chute, were endorsed and the references were obtained. Books had to be purchased, cataloged, cross-referenced, and put away. Microfilm had to be stored. Quietly dressed men with a fresh college look about them sat at the long reading desks studying thick volumes and making notes. The silence was cavernous. Only outside the doors could the distant whirring of the computers in the basement be heard.

For some time before the news of the Watmough bequest was officially confirmed, word of it had filtered down to us. Milly Fellowes, the librarian, had had an inkling, and that in itself was as good an indication as any. Milly Fellowes was not one to be fanciful or to treat anything but with the utmost seriousness.

"Sir Charles and Jules Barthelmy were men of like minds," she had told me shortly after the announcement came. We had been sitting in the staff canteen, and Milly was clearly excited. I remembered she had had cheesecake with her coffee. "Men of vision, who had a sense of what was right and proper. They were long-standing friends. Jules Barthelmy was such a fine man." Her fork had faltered briefly over the cheesecake.

Her loyalty to the financier had been unquestioned, even after his death. She had been with him in the days long before the foundation was established. Most of her life had been devoted to the cause of Jules Barthelmy and his wide-ranging empire that had made him a millionaire many times over. He had been a man of vast reputation, of decided political views, and was a power to be reckoned with. He had been dead three years at the time I joined the Institute.

Milly didn't often talk about the early days, or about Jules Barthelmy, but when she did, her eyes animated behind her thick glasses, her voice quickening, I listened avidly in an attempt to establish in my mind a more or less complete picture of the man. But the more I read about him or heard about him, the more elusive he became. Even in the rare photographs that were available, there was the same chameleonlike quality, so that he never looked the same in any two of them. I had the impression that it was a cloak he had deliberately drawn around him, an air of mystery that he possibly relished. Even when Milly talked about him, the picture, if anything, became still more confused. He was a small gnomelike man whose origins were obscure and whose power was enormous—that was practically all I knew about him.

"There was always the feeling that the Watmough Collection would come to us one day, after probate had been passed," Milly had said. "It really is marvelous. Quite wonderful. The best of its kind anywhere in the world." Her cheeks had been flushed, and the cheesecake forgotten. "Just think of it, the finest complete interpretations of the *hadith* commentaries, including—you know this—the Bokhara Commentary, a treasure, truly a treasure. A storehouse, Ali. Pre-Islamic poetry, the Ummayad and Abbasid periods, scientific and philosophical treatises from the Toledo scholars, and on, and on, representing the very cream of Arab thought and culture. But the Bokhara Commentary alone would be enough. There has been so much controversy surrounding it."

As I turned into High Holborn and walked under the heavy gray London sky toward the Underground at the corner of Kingsway, I thought back to Milly as she had been that lunchtime in the canteen, looking so much younger in her animation. The dryness that was the impression she had conveyed to people, and which seemed so apposite to a woman in advanced middle age who lived alone and whose only passion in life was books, had completely gone. It was only books that had brought her to life. The next time I had seen her, she had been preoccupied and uncommunicative. It was the last time I had seen her.

As I thought about Milly, I felt sad. By rights, she should have been here, in London, instead of me, on her way up to the Watmough family seat in Shropshire to catalog the collection and make the arrangements to have it shipped back to Chicago. She would have known exactly what she was doing, whereas I felt myself to be too young and inexperienced to do the job properly. I certainly didn't feel the confidence our section head, Sam Warren, had shown in me. A simple inventory, he had said. A piece of cake. The sky seemed grayer and lower. Everything looked gray, even the faces of the people who crowded the pavements. The traffic moved slowly. Horns sounded. High square black taxis maneuvered ably; the lumbering red double-decker buses were full. Milly had been looking forward to visiting London for the first time.

At the corner, I hesitated outside the Underground station, then decided to walk some more. I had seen hardly anything at all of London, and if James Montague was driving me up to Shropshire in the morning, there wasn't much time for sightseeing. Perhaps after I had finished my work at Ravenswood, I thought, I might be able to spare a day or two for that on my way back to the States. I didn't know how long I would be at Ravenswood; I still didn't have a clear idea of the enormity of the task. I turned down Kingsway toward Aldwych and the Strand. I could see something of the city at least before I returned to the hotel for what I hoped would be an early night.

The streets were crowded. Everybody seemed to be in a hurry. Knots formed at the Underground entrances, where newspaper sellers stood beside placards proclaiming the news headlines in roughly drawn characters. I walked on, not quite sure where I was going. When I felt I had walked enough, I would take a cab back to the hotel. Sometimes I stopped and looked in shop windows. The red buses roared past in seemingly endless procession, and the cold air made my face tingle.

I walked aimlessly, turning up into Covent Garden and through to Charing Cross Road, absorbing the great city and its constant movement, its strangeness. I felt apprehensive, and a little homesick. The city crowded around me yet I wasn't part of it. I moved on toward Leicester Square and Piccadilly, past the theaters and restaurants and department stores. I was jostled once or twice, but I hardly noticed. Once, when I glimpsed my reflection in a shop window, I smiled in recognition at the fair-haired girl in the beige belted raincoat, and thought: Just what are *you* doing here in such a place? Partly reassured, I walked more quickly.

"It couldn't have happened at a worse time, believe you me," Sam Warren had said on the afternoon of the day we had heard about Milly, and I was still in a state of stunned disbelief. "On top of everything else, this oil crisis, the staff shortage, we've never been so busy—and now this has happened." Sam was concerned, he had toyed with his glasses. The sound of the computer had thrummed up through the floor. "There's nothing else for it, Ali. You'll have to go to England. There's no time. We have to get that collection sorted out and over here as soon as possible. In fact, we've only got to the end of the month. I'm sorry, Ali, but that's the way it is. Those are my instructions. We don't have any choice in the matter, I'm afraid. You'll have to go. We just don't have anyone else."

The days that had followed were so rushed, so frantic, that I hardly had time to think. I had passed through them in a kind of trance. Even when the plane was taking off from O'Hare, I still couldn't believe it was happening.

There was a hoarding around the statue of Eros in Piccadilly Circus. Different aromas drifted over me, Tandoori chicken, pizza, gasoline. The clothes in the shops along Piccadilly were expensive. Young people were selling jewelry and leather goods from makeshift stalls, and paintings were propped up against the railings of Green Park. It seemed to me that just about all the nationalities of the world were represented in these teeming streets, as if London were a crucible in which they were all compounded to form the inimitable character of the city. Fragments of a babble of tongues fell down around me like the leaves from the trees in the park. A group of stately, slow-moving Africans in national costume looked at me blandly as I passed them. Pigeons fluttered in the eaves of the tall gray buildings.

On the plane, I had read and reread the thick folder of mimeographed sheets Sam Warren had handed me. It was a complete bibliography, with a brief rundown on the more important manuscripts, including the Bokhara Commentary about which Milly had been so excited and which was undoubtedly the most important item in the Watmough Collection. I had tried to get the feel of the collection before I had even seen it, but it was impossible to break through the barrier presented by the endless lists of titles and dates, the explanations and footnotes. The typed letters and figures had swirled through my head, disjointed, without coherence or form. They had made my eyes tired, and I had put them down.

In the park, people were throwing crumbs to the ducks and swans in the pond. I turned up toward Buckingham Palace.

On top of, or perhaps part of, the apprehension I felt about the task into which I had been so abruptly thrust was the suspicion that it was not quite as simple as it had been made out. For instance, there was the urgency to have the collection brought back to Chicago. It was the Institute's top priority, so much so that they were prepared to send me, comparatively inexperienced, to England to make the necessary arrangements. I had sensed the urgency. Sam Warren had himself been clearly apprehensive, and I was almost certain that there was more to the assignment than met the eye. It was a damned shame that right on the very eve of her departure for England, Milly Fellowes should have been run down and killed instantly by a car that didn't stop. It was sheer bad luck.

I stared at the massive facade of Buckingham Palace, the immobile sentries in their red coats and busbies, the policemen at the gate, at the elaborate Queen Victoria Memorial where the tree-lined Mall opened into the place in front of the palace, at the milling tourists, and thought that tomorrow I would be looking at another type of mansion. Milly had told me that Ravenswood dated back to the days of the Tudors. I began to walk down Constitution Hill, following the high wall that shielded the palace garden from the public gaze. I felt I had walked enough.

In Knightsbridge I hailed a cab and gave the driver the address of my hotel. Five minutes later we turned off Cromwell Road into a long curving street of Regency terrace houses and pulled up outside the Wilton Private Hotel, behind a sleek black Rolls-Royce limousine with tinted windows through which I could just make out the outlines of two men in the rear and a uniformed chauffeur at the wheel. I paid the driver then, as it swung out from the curb, began to walk past the Rolls-Royce toward the steps that led up from the pavement to the hotel entrance.

I was just coming abreast of the limousine when, suddenly, the rear door opened and a man in a neat dark business suit stepped out to confront me. I was swerving to avoid him when he grabbed my arm just above the elbow, his strong fingers digging mercilessly into my flesh. I gasped and tried to pull away, but he was dragging me to the car. I cried out. There was an elusive smell of sweet tobacco. The engine started, and then I was flung heavily into the car. My knees hit the floor and I sprawled across the seat, my face buried in rich-smelling leather. The man slid in beside me. The door slammed, and the car eased out into the street. The whole incident hadn't taken more than ten seconds. There had been no time to scream or to do anything desperate.

3

"Jamil is a true son of the desert. He is not always understood." The voice was soft and accented. Hands reached beneath my arms and pulled me up from my kneeling position on the floor onto the seat. My arm was still hurting where my assailant's fingers had dug into it. "You mustn't be afraid. We are not terrorists. All we seek from you is some conversation, which I hope may prove mutually profitable."

I sat on the edge of the seat. Through the darkened windows the rows of terraces slid silently past. The uniformed chauffeur was separated from the rear by a sliding glass panel. The iron railings of a private park that divided the street streaked rapidly past us like a blurred series of exclamation marks.

"What do you want with me?" I was only just beginning to get my breath back.

"An arrangement, if that is possible."

He sat in the corner, a slightly built sallow man of indeterminate age, with dark thinning hair and an aquiline nose. His large brown liquid eyes stared solemnly back at me. I tried not to show him I was frightened, but I don't know how successful the attempt was. I was still trying to collect my thoughts. All I knew was that I had been abducted in broad daylight, forced into the car, and driven away. But why me? What did they want with me? To hold me hostage—to what advantage? It didn't make sense. No one knew me in London, and I was hardly any sort of bargaining counter. The only explanation, it seemed to me in those first few confused moments, with the smell of leather mingling with sweet tobacco and pomade, as the car picked up speed, was that I had been mistaken for someone else.

"You've made a mistake. You've got the wrong person."

"Not at all." The thin man leaned forward and butted his cigarette in the ashtray. His lips stretched in a wan smile. "Despite the unfortunate impression that might have been created by Jamil's method of introduction, we are really quite civilized people. Jamil was just a little . . . eager, that's all. However, the approach was direct enough. Any other might have aroused your suspicions and prompted a reluctance to participate in this conference."

I glanced at the man who was sitting on my other side. He was young and swarthy, with a thin straggly mustache, a pocked complexion, and very white teeth.

"No, Miss Baker, I haven't made a mistake," the other man went on. "I know who you are and why you are in England. It is, of course, very pertinent. It is at this point our interests coincide."

With a sinking sensation I stared at him. "I don't understand you at all."

"You will, you will."

The car's engine was barely audible. We stopped at a set of traffic lights, and I weighed my chances of escape. But they didn't look good. I was hemmed in by the two men, and I would have no hope of reaching either of the doors, which I suspected were locked, anyway. If I screamed, it was unlikely anyone would hear me before I was quickly silenced. Jamil grinned at me knowingly, as if he were following the train of my thoughts. The smell of the pomade with which his thick wavy hair had been slicked down was sickly-sweet and cloying.

SECRET AT RAVENSWOOD

The lights changed and we were moving again.

My fright was fast giving way to anger. I had walked farther than I had intended, and now I was tired. I had been looking forward to dinner and an early night. I was certainly in no mood for riddles or games of any sort.

"Let me out at once!" I cried, twisting around on the plush leather seat again to glare at the thin man. On my other side, Jamil laid one hand on my arm. I shook it away. The driver changed lanes, cutting in between a taxi and a bus. I groped for words that would sound forceful and threatening, but somehow they lacked conviction. It was all so unreal. The traffic moved around us, so close yet so far removed from us. "I mean it. If you're not kidnapping me . . ." It sounded so stupid. Of course they were kidnapping me. I should be struggling more, making a scene, but somehow, for a reason I was unable to fathom, I believed him. I didn't think he meant to hurt me. He looked rather timid. Jamil looked positively friendly.

We turned up Palace Gate, then into Kensington Road. The gardens stretched away to our left. The thin man reached forward from the comfortable depths of the seat and tapped against the glass partition. The chauffeur pulled over to the side of the street and stopped the car. The thin man sighed.

"I think, if you have no objection, we will

take a stroll through the park. It is quiet at this time of day. We will be private."

Jamil opened the door on his side and stepped out onto the pavement. He held the door open as I climbed out of the car with the thin man following me. A short distance along the footpath a short queue of people was waiting at a bus stop, and I thought if I cried for help now, or made a run for it, I might just have a chance. But I couldn't be too positive about that. Jamil was standing very close to me, and I was sure that if I so much as looked as if I were about to make a dash for it, he would grab me before I could make that move. There was something very alert and pantherlike about the way he was watching me. I knew how quick he was.

The thin man stood beside me, his hands thrust into the pockets of his dark blue overcoat. He nodded toward the park gate. "Come, shall we walk?" he said, beginning to move across the pavement. More curious now than frightened or even annoyed, I followed him. When we reached the gate, I glanced back at the car, which I saw was standing within the double yellow lines of a no-parking zone. Then I noticed the diplomatic plates. Jamil was walking slowly behind us.

Dusk was rapidly closing in across the park, and a light mist was forming among the trees. In the deceptive gray light the grass was a very pale washed-out green. On the far side of the park, the traffic moved in a steady stream along Bayswater Road, and there were lights showing in the windows of Kensington Palace, which closed off the western end of the park. Our footsteps sounded on the path as we walked for some yards in silence. Jamil followed a short distance behind us. Still with his hands in the pockets of his overcoat, my companion was staring straight ahead of him, his high forehead furrowed by a small frown of concentration. He walked with small, precise steps, and I noticed how small his highly polished black shoes were.

"Who are you?" I asked at last.

"My name is Khamal," he replied. "It is not relevant. It is not on my own behalf that this approach has been made to you."

There weren't many people in the park. The benches were unoccupied. "Well, who then?" I demanded. "Why?"

He stopped on the path and swung to face me. His eyes were still solemn. "I will come to the point," he said. "You are here in connection with the Watmough Collection. I am authorized by my . . . I am authorized to enter into negotiations with you."

"What sort of negotiations?"

We faced each other on the path. Jamil had also stopped. Taking his hands from his pockets, Khamal reached inside his coat and produced a soft leather cigarette case. He opened it and took out a short oval cigarette, which he lit with a gold lighter.

"Twenty-five thousand United States dollars is a considerable sum of money," he said, exhaling a cloud of sweet-smelling smoke. "I'm sure there is much you could do with it." The mist was rising between the trees. Khamal glanced at his wristwatch. "They will be closing the gates soon."

We began to walk again, with Jamil bringing up the rear. The aromatic smoke from Khamal's cigarette drifted across to me. "You said you would come to the point," I prompted him.

"I mentioned twenty-five thousand dollars. I also mentioned an arrangement."

The shadows were closing in. We crossed an intersecting path, then turned onto another that led to a round shallow pond. "You seem to me to be an intelligent girl," Khamal went on in his softly accented voice. "And I do say there is no risk attached. A simple matter of misplacement, with no question of blame."

We stopped at the edge of the pond. Khamal finished his cigarette and flicked the butt across the breeze-ruffled surface of the water. He turned to me. "You have heard, of course, of the so-called Bokhara Commentary?"

"Of course."

"Then you know something of its history.

SECRET AT RAVENSWOOD

You know that it has a certain . . . theological significance."

"I suppose it does," I said hesitantly. "I know some people consider it to be a hoax."

Khamal shrugged. "There are always schools of thought. On such matters of interpretation, there is always dissension, interpretations of the interpretation, splitting hairs. And there's always somebody to cry hoax. Look at your own Christianity, and the schisms that developed *there*. It's the same with any religion. But be that as it may, whether the Commentary is a hoax or not, the point remains that it does represent a certain cohesive element, particularly in these times of revolutionary change and fervor." He looked at me hopefully. "You understand my meaning?"

Jamil was standing motionless at the junction of the paths. Fallen leaves stirred in the rising breeze. "All I understand is that you're offering me twenty-five thousand dollars for the Bokhara Commentary."

"In a nutshell, yes."

"I haven't even seen it."

"You soon will."

"But I'm not in a position to do what you're asking," I protested. "Even if I *were* interested, and I'm not. The entire collection has to go back to Chicago, and the Bokhara Commentary forms an essential part of the collection. There's the small matter of security, for one thing."

"We are prepared to extend the offer."

"Who's we?"

Staring down at the murky water of the pond, he seemed to consider this for a few moments. When he looked up again, his expression was quite serene. "It is only in the past month that the document has assumed an almost crucial importance for us. Yes. Perhaps you have already guessed. I do believe you are intelligent. Perhaps you are already ahead of me."

I wasn't, but I said nothing. Khamal went on. "What happened in Iran is only the beginning. My own country now . . . We are in the middle of *jihad*, holy war, the cause of Islam sweeping down at all levels. These are exciting times." He paused and stared back down at the water again. "It is a force no one can resist. The impetus is too overwhelming. It is a spiritual force, you see. Everyone is caught up in it, and the forces of reaction are powerless. I mean, among other things, your Institute and what it represents. Oh, yes, forces of reaction. A select band of men like Jules Barthelmy and Sir Charles Watmough, and others, men of power, imperialist in outlook and dedicated to preserve the status quo, propping up corrupt regimes through massive infusions of money and weapons. Politics, oil, big business, spheres of influence—it's all so very difficult." He turned away from the pond and began to walk back along the path toward the gate. I walked with him. "I'm telling you this only because I want you to understand that there is much at stake. There is also a question of justice, and in these troubled times the document does provide an emotional focus."

We strolled past Jahil, who was standing on the grass to one side of the path, watching us. I wondered if he were armed, and guessed he must be. He looked very capable. "I don't know about politics or religion, or justice," I said. "They are not my concern. I have a job to do." As soon as I said it, I realized I had sounded rather prim and self-important. I remembered how I had become carried away in James Montague's office, when I had talked in sweeping terms of justice and rightful ownership, which, given half a chance, could just as easily have encompassed a spectrum of moral attitudes. Quickly I aired something else that had been bothering me from the time my companion had begun to make himself understood. "How did you know who I am?" I asked. "Where I worked, and where I'm staying in London? You seem to know a lot about me."

His brief smile made him look tired. He seemed to be carrying a heavy weight on his shoulders. He stopped again and faced me. The smile was gone, but he still looked tired. "You will not help us?" he asked.

I shook my head. "I can't."

He sighed heavily. "I can see you are a determined young lady," he said quietly. "Perhaps you will be persuaded? My offer does not tempt you?"

"I told you . . ."

His voice sharpened, and it was as if the liquid in his large, expressive, almost womanish eyes had suddenly congealed. "All right, as you wish, but you are really being foolish. You are not serving yourself in any way. It is unfortunate. Once before we appealed to reason, but to no avail. We encountered a similar stubbornness. . . . Still, perhaps your refusal need not be final. I will give you some time to think it over." He smiled again, his eyes softened again. "I'm sure you will come to see reason. You will see that it is a much wiser course to take. Now I shall take you back to your hotel."

"No, thank you," I said. "I would prefer to walk."

"As you wish. It will give you time to think."

I stood on the path and watched him walk briskly toward the Palace Gate. As Jamil moved across the grass to catch up with him, he looked across at me and grinned widely. His teeth gleamed in the gathering gloom. It seemed to me to underline what I now recognized had been a threat, put to me in courteous, almost sugary terms, but no less a threat because of that. As I stared after the two receding figures, I realized I was caught up in something that

SECRET AT RAVENSWOOD

would soon have me floundering well out of my depth. The breeze caught a sheet of newspaper and sent it fluttering across the path. I began to shiver, and it wasn't only because of the cold.

4

The Wilton Private Hotel had an air of shabby gentility. The heating was inadequate, the pipes in the bathrooms made strange rumbling noises. Dusty potted plants crowded the narrow lobby and were dotted around the lounge that opened off it. There were cane tables and lumpy overstuffed armchairs and sofas patterned with faded flowery prints. The carpet was threadbare and there was a picture of the queen on horseback. The place carried an air of being an outpost. It was the sort of es-

SECRET AT RAVENSWOOD

tablishment favored by elderly people of independent but limited means, a fair sampling of whom were always to be found in the lounge playing cards; reading newspapers, periodicals, or books borrowed from the public library; dozing; or just staring into space. There was an overall atmosphere of ossification. It was very quiet, and even the desultory communication that passed between these mostly permanent occupants had an ancient, cobwebby feel to it. It was as if they were all waiting for something to happen, yet knowing it wouldn't. The expectation had become lackluster and restricted. I had wondered why Chicago had booked me into such a place, and decided it must have been due to budget considerations. The food was atrocious.

Aware of a dozen pairs of eyes watching me from the lounge, I walked across the lobby to the desk. The clerk, elderly and stooped, and a shade more cheerful than most of the guests, looked up from his newspaper.

"'Evening, miss," he greeted me, putting down the newspaper and reaching up for my key from one of the pigeonholes on the wall behind him. "There was someone looking for you earlier," he told me, inclining his head a little so that the light gleamed palely on the hairless dome of his head. "A gent. A foreigner." His bleary eyes fixed on me, as if challenging me to deny the veracity of his statement. From his tone, I gathered he didn't care much for foreigners.

I picked up the key to my room. "Yes, yes, I know."

He was still watching me, obviously waiting for me to elaborate, to satisfy the curiosity that must have been with him from the time the inquiry was made. "Seemed to be in a hurry. He looked quite annoyed when I told him you weren't here. Put out, like. I told him what you told me, that you would be back in time for dinner. Later in the afternoon, you said. He said he'd wait, but he must have changed his mind, eh?"

I turned away from the desk. Opposite me, in an alcove flanked by two drooping aspidistras, was a pay telephone. I was undecided, and after my encounter with Khamal, still shaken. I had walked quickly back to the hotel, nervously, with the feeling that I was surrounded by menace. The people I had passed in the street represented in some way a threat. From any one of the slow-moving cars or buses, I had half-expected someone to emerge and grab hold of me. Even now, back in the hotel, I didn't feel safe.

I didn't know what to do. I stared at the telephone. I could put a call through to Sam Warren in Chicago and explain what had happened. He would tell me what I should do. He would probably reassure me and tell me not to worry.

SECRET AT RAVENSWOOD

It was lunchtime in Chicago, and he probably wouldn't be back in his office for another hour or so. I could place the call and tell him about Khamal's offer for the Bokhara Commentary, and his implied determination not to be put off by my refusal to cooperate. But if I did that, I thought, it would not be on this phone among the listless foliage of the hotel lobby. It was much too public. Even if the connection were good, I would have to raise my voice to make myself heard over such a distance. I would be easily overheard. No, if I were to call Sam, it would have to be from somewhere more private. I thought of James Montague, and realized it was more than probable that he had already left his office. I could try, of course, on the off chance that he was working late. But what could I tell him? I didn't know. I was totally confused. Apart from Sam Warren back in Chicago, there was really no one else to whom I could turn. It was still too close to me. Perhaps, in the morning, when I was on my way up to Ravenswood, and indeed at the house itself, the incident would not seem nearly so important. I was jittery, that was all.

"The dinner gong will be going in ten minutes, miss," the clerk called behind me.

"Thanks."

Enclosed by the musty smell of damp clothes and boiled cabbage, I climbed the narrow stairs to my room on the second floor. In the time I had had to think about what had transpired in that space of no more than half an hour I had been with Khamal, I realized that what worried me most—more than the offer itself and his suggestion that that was not to be the end of the matter—was how much he had known about me. He had known where I was staying in London, and had been able to recognize me as I was about to turn into the hotel, which showed, I thought, an enormous amount of confidence. He hadn't struck me as one who was in the habit of making mistakes. Taking it further, it meant he had been thoroughly briefed about me, was familiar with my physical appearance, which made me suspect he had been supplied with a photograph of me. The last photograph that had been taken of me had been when I joined the Institute. Two copies had been needed for the files, and another for the identification plate we all had to wear inside the building. To have the pictures taken, I had had to walk to the other side of the building, along a labyrinthine series of passageways and past a series of heavy metal doors. The studio had been behind another metal door.

On the hotel landing I stood to one side to allow two old ladies, one of them with a walking stick, to pass me on their way downstairs. I returned their greeting and continued on up the stairs. The electric light at the top of the staircase was dim and flickering.

SECRET AT RAVENSWOOD

In the poor light of the passage, I unlocked the door of my room and stepped inside. I switched on the light. The smell of boiled cabbage and raincoats was still with me; it seemed to have permeated every part of the building—the walls, the floor, the ceiling. The room was cold. I looked around and saw that everything was as I had left it. I don't know why I thought, no matter how vaguely, it might have been otherwise.

The room was economically furnished. There was an iron bedstead with a lumpy mattress and a pea-green quilted cover, a bedside table, a wardrobe, a washstand, and a gas fire that needed an inexhaustible supply of coins in the slot to keep it going. It was the same with the hot-water system in the communal bathroom at the end of the passage. I hadn't quite mastered it; it made me nervous.

Crossing to the wardrobe, I took out my briefcase and returned to the bed. I sat down, and opening the case, took out the thick folder and opened it on my lap. I shuffled through the papers until I found the sheets that dealt with the Bokhara Commentary. I began to read them again, my eyes scanning the closely typed pages, looking for the answer. The dinner gong reverberated dully below me, but I ignored it.

When Milly Fellowes had told me the Bokhara Commentary was controversial, she had been guilty of an understatement; its discovery during the latter part of the nineteenth century had created a furor. Its revelations attacked the very foundation of Islamic belief. It was the cause of prolonged and bitter theological dispute, of claim and counterclaim, and the inevitable and almost deafening cry of hoax. Scholars had examined and expounded, tests had been exhaustive, and nothing was positively resolved.

The major disputation about the document revolved around its author, purported to be Al-Bokhari, the great Muslim traditionalist whose authority rated in importance second only to the Koran itself. A native of the Central Asian city of Bokhara, the ninth-century theologian was the greatest interpreter of the writings and utterances of the prophet Muhammad, and his dicta had been accepted unquestioningly by the *sunni,* or orthodox Muslims who comprise the vast majority of that faith. Al-Bokhari's writings were cut and dried, interpretations that brooked no interpretation. For many centuries his theological place was assured. Then, in the form of the Bokhara Commentary, came the bombshell.

Briefly, this document, supposedly written by Al-Bokhari in the exile to which he had been banished as a result of a disagreement over the divine origins of the writings in the Holy Book, amended certain of his earlier interpretations, particularly in regard to the succession to the prophet Muhammad. It was slippery stuff, and very involved, but in essence it gave credence to the claim of the followers of Ali, the fourth caliph, Muhammad's son-in-law, that the succession was rightly his, which forms the basis of the *shi'a* branch of Muhammadanism. This branch, comprising about one-tenth of the number of adherents to the faith, flourishes particularly in Iran, Iraq, and certain other countries in the region. The Commentary—it was really a form of apologia—had become a rallying point for the *shi'as*, who had declared it as proof positive of the legality of their claim. Al-Bokhari was such an unimpeachable authority, after all. Then the accusations began. Loud claims were made that the document was a forgery, and these gathered some credence over the years. The argument had spread to the streets. There had been riots, assassinations, and a small desert war.

Somehow, after the First World War, the Commentary had found its way from Bokhara to Baghdad, where Sir Charles Watmough, who was British ambassador at the time, had eventually managed to acquire it. How he achieved this was not stated, but he did obtain it and take it back to England, and it wasn't until many years later, until after his retirement, that that fact became known, by which time the controversy had subsided.

Now it seemed that interest in the document

had been revived after all those years. It had become important to someone, at least, and I didn't know why. Khamal had mentioned Iran, recently overtaken by a *shi'a*-inspired revolution, and referred to his own country, which he hadn't named, and the fact that it was in the middle of a holy war. It didn't take much to guess which country that was, succumbing to the movement which had already engulfed neighboring Iran. What the so-called Bokhara Commentary had to do with that revolution, I didn't know. Nor did the brief synopsis I was reading now help me much.

"Hoax or not," Milly had said, "the fact remains that a lot of people were killed because of it."

Closing the folder, I replaced it in the briefcase, then stood up. I decided to freshen up a little before going down to dinner.

5

James Montague was late. It was almost nine-thirty when he bounded up the steps and into the hotel lobby, where, surrounded by foliage, I was waiting for him. He began to apologize profusely. He told me he had overslept. Picking up my bag, he carried it out to the car, which, from the top of the steps, I saw was a small battered and mud-stained Mini Minor. He opened the door, slung my bag onto the back seat, and grinned up at me. He was dressed casually in a thick chocolate sweater, beige corduroy trousers, and desert boots.

I could still taste the egg and bacon I had had for breakfast. The bacon had been more than crispy; it had been close to charcoal. The egg had been filmy. I hadn't finished it.

"Ready to go, then," James called up to me. "We're all packed."

Still looking doubtfully at the tiny boxlike car, I moved down the steps to the pavement. The sun was shining, the sky blue and cloudless, and there was a crisp bite in the air. It was a pleasant day. There were quite a number of people abroad on the street, and the curving row of terrace houses presented an identical front.

I hadn't slept well at all. I had tossed and turned on the lumpy mattress, my mind a turmoil of racing, fragmented thoughts. There had been Khamal and the Bokhara Commentary, a sheet of newspaper fluttering across the path in the park, Jamil's white smile, the shallow pond, and gaudily dressed Africans. There had been Milly Fellowes with something obviously on her mind. I had listened for sounds, and there had been so many of them—the gurgling pipes, footsteps in the passage outside, doors opening and closing, murmured good nights, and even later, after most of the other guests had gone to bed, I had still lain awake listening. A man in one of the adjoining rooms had had a bad hacking cough that had gone on for most of the night. There had been creaking and rustling sounds. I had listened to the traffic outside. I had been nervous, and had made sure the door was locked. I had had the feeling I was being watched.

Even at dinner the night before, I had looked carefully around the room, surreptitiously observing the other diners. Any one of them, I had thought, could have been there for the sole purpose of keeping an eye on me, even the tweedy, florid-faced man with the broken purple veins in his nose and cheeks who sat at my table, whom I had earlier heard addressed as Major, who had reeked of gin, who had leered at me and called me "m'dear," talked wistfully of India, and had inadvertently put his elbow in the tapioca pudding. It could even have been one of the card-playing old ladies, or the dough-faced waitress who had managed to slop some of the lukewarm mulligatawny soup on the tablecloth as she was placing it in front of me. It could have been anyone. I had bravely plowed through a monstrosity winsomely called toad-in-the-hole which turned out to be a sausage cooked in batter and which was accompanied by watery cabbage, mashed potatoes, and baby carrots, all of which had only served to increase my nervousness. It could have been the quiet man reading a racing newspaper in the corner of the room near the serving hatch. My sleep, when it came, had been desultory and unsatisfying, and I was just as tired as I had been the night before.

In the car, I could feel the seat springs digging into me. James started the car, and there was an ugly grating sound as he put it into gear. The car lurched out from the curb, and immediately there was an agonized screech of tires, a furious blasting of a car's horn, someone yelling. James waved to the other driver in friendly acknowledgment, called "Much obliged," and we were on our way. I settled back on the seat and tried to make myself comfortable.

We drove through the streets, diving in and out of the traffic with such daring that I found myself holding on to the rim of the dashboard and silently willing him to take it a little easier. His conversation was light and breezy, and I wondered if I should tell him about my meeting with Khamal the night before. The question was lodged within me like a heavy and unmalleable lump of clay, as indigestible as last night's dinner. I felt I needed to tell somebody about it, but I wasn't sure *whom* I should tell, or whom I should trust. If Milly Fellowes were still alive . . . If she were still alive, I wouldn't be having this problem. I glanced across at James, his hair stirring in the breeze that came in through the open window, and although he was friendly enough and I decided I could probably trust him, something held me back. He, too, had known my movements, had known where I was staying, and would have been able to provide a fairly detailed description of me—long blond hair, blue eyes, a beige raincoat . . . an English rose. After I had left his office, he could easily have picked up the telephone, dialed a number . . . I shook my head. It was too silly. All the same, I remained on my guard.

We drove past rows and rows of suburban semi-detached villas with neatly laid-out gardens, past apartment complexes and parks. Gradually the houses gave way to open country, and we were on the motorway heading northwest. We passed fields and forests, the sunlight washing them into soft shades of red, orange, and gold, rising from a carpet of fallen rust-colored leaves. The air smelled good. London slipped away behind us, and I began to feel a little more relaxed.

James was driving very fast, and the tiny car vibrated all around me. The seat springs dug into me. He looked across at me. "Penny for 'em."

"What?"

"Your thoughts."

"Oh."

"You look preoccupied."

We passed the Birmingham turnoff. We moved out to overtake a semitrailer that was belching out a cloud of black smoke. "Just a little tired," I told him. "I didn't sleep very well."

"I called Lady Watmough last night," he said. "She's expecting us sometime after lunch, so I thought we'd stop somewhere for a bite. The old girl's having a few people up for the weekend. She's a great one for hunting and fishing, an outdoors type. It must be the last hunt of the season. To hounds, a good-luck toast from the stirrup cup, tantivy and tally-ho, the scent of the fox, and the unspeakable in full pursuit of the uneatable. I wish you luck. There'll be a lot of noise. It mightn't be so easy to concentrate."

Villages and farms flashed past us. Green hills began to roll away on either side of us. Streams sparkled in the sunlight. There were towns and tall smokestacks. There were billboards—"Guinness is good for you"—and overpasses. Before Wolverhampton, we turned off the motorway and headed west. The countryside became more hilly and picturesque. We wound down a hillside into a valley, and crossed a river before climbing again.

We had lunch at a pub in an old market town called Bridgenorth, set on a cliff above the River Severn, the walls of which still bore the scars of a Cromwell bombardment three centuries earlier, when the castle that occupied the site had been completely destroyed. James had turned the car off the cobbled main street through an archway into the courtyard adjoining the pub.

Sitting in one corner of the dining room next to a window that looked out over the sharply sloping main street of the town, we ate roast-beef sandwiches and shared a bottle of Beaujolais. A low buzz of conversation came from the smoke-filled bar next door, through which we had had to pass to reach the dining room. The hills ranged away to the west, and the sunlight slanted through the windows onto the starched white tablecloth.

"Tell me about the Institute," James said. "Did you go straight there from college?"

"Yes. It was arranged through the student vocational body." I remembered the sad-faced man who had interviewed me in the dean's office, and how closely he had watched me as he asked me questions, as if he were more interested in my reactions to them than in the answers themselves. Some of the questions had struck me as rather strange. He had wanted to know my involvement in student politics. I had told him I had had none, and had the impression that he had already known the answer. The impression had been there when he had asked me about my family. He had already known my father had been with the State Department in Washington.

"You're not worried about this thing, are you?" James was leaning forward with his arms folded on the table. His gray eyes somberly studied me. I managed a smile.

"Not at all. Why do you say that?"

He shrugged. "I don't know. I get the impression that you're not very happy about the job in hand."

"It was all rather sudden," I said. "I just hope I know what I'm doing."

He picked up the wine bottle and refilled my glass. The sunlight made the red liquid look smoky. "I'm sure you will. As you say, it *was* rather sudden, and unfortunate. . . . I mean, the accident. We had a telegram. Did you know her well?"

"Milly? Well enough, I guess. She wasn't what you would call an outgoing person. She was very good to me, and she did take her responsibilities very seriously. She was really looking forward to coming to England."

James slowly shook his head. "That's bad luck."

"It was very quick," I said. "She wouldn't have known what happened."

His cheeks were slightly flushed. He looked quite healthy and fresh. He even seemed more capable somehow. "Look," he said earnestly, "if there's anything you need, if you need any help, if there's anything . . . I'm staying the weekend with friends at Shrewsbury. It's not far from Ravenswood, about a half-hour's drive. I'll give you the number. If there's anything at all, call me and I'll come over." He sat back on his chair and smiled easily. "Maybe I'll come over anyway and see you. I'll be a friendly, reassuring face. We can go for long country rambles. I'll be going back to London on Monday, and then you'll have all the time you need."

I was pleased with the suggestion. I had the feeling I would be in need of a friendly, reassuring face, and I really was growing to like him. I sipped my wine and looked out at the street. The shops were small, and people greeted each other on the footpath. Everything seemed so leisurely. James took a pen from his pocket and scribbled a telephone number on the back of a beer coaster. "Slip this into your bag," he said, sliding the coaster across the table at me. "That's where you can reach me."

Taking the beer coaster, I glanced at the number, then dropped it into my bag. "Why do you think I might be in need of help?" I asked.

"You never know," he replied with a laugh. "The Black Baron might grab you."

"The Black Baron?"

"The resident ghost. Old Sir Mondrath himself being restless and rattling his chains. He was the one who built the manor, back in fourteen-something. The story goes that he still haunts the place, lets out bloodcurdling oaths, and generally makes a nuisance of himself. A popular legend. I think the family is rather fond of him."

"Oh," I said.

"Perhaps thinking you might need my help," he went on, "is just wishful thinking. I'm the eternal optimist."

Just then a small dark car drove past the window, and I caught a brief glimpse of the driver's face. There was something vaguely and disturbingly familiar about it. The car was gone, but the almost subliminal glimpse I had had of that face remained with me. It had been a swarthy face, and had borne a strong resemblance to Jamil, the man who had pushed me into the back of the Rolls-Royce outside my London hotel and had stood guard while Khamal had walked with me in the park and become enthused about spiritual regeneration. I told myself I was mistaken. It was someone who had looked like Jamil, that was all. A coincidence.

"Is anything the matter?"

I started. "Nothing."

"You were miles away."

Ten minutes later we were driving out of the town, along narrow hedge-lined roads that curved around the hills. The villages we passed were smaller and farther apart. I felt much better. I was enjoying James's company.

"Did you know Sir Charles?" I asked.

"Not really," he replied. "All his business was handled by the senior partners, Grahame in particular. They were good friends. There was this sort of club thing to which they both belonged, very conservative. You know, politics over port and a cigar. One of the old school, colonial administrator and all that. Quite brilliant, I believe. Crusty, I suppose, and set in his ways. Spent most of his life abroad, mainly in the Middle East, his special area of interest. He served his country well."

We came to a crossroads and turned right. The road was narrow, with barely enough room for two cars to pass. It wound between the hedges. The trees rose tall above us. There were fields and wooden gates, stone walls, grazing sheep, a red mailbox sitting incongruously in the middle of nowhere, muted shades. We climbed another hill, and the country undulated away around us.

We came to an old neglected lodge at the fork of another road that led sharply up to our left. We turned into the fork and began to negotiate the steep climb. The road was bumpy and uneven, and the trees closed above us so that the road was dappled with pale sunlight and heavy shadow. Fallen leaves were scattered across the road, and the engine of the tiny car whined and strained as we climbed still higher.

"Not long to go now," James said. "We're almost there."

The trees closed thickly in around us, and now there was more shadow than sunlight. The slope began to even out, and the trees began to thin out from the edge of the road. We came to the summit of the hill.

"There she is," James said.

Ahead of us was another, higher hill. I stared at it and the mansion that crowned it. It was my first view of Ravenswood.

6

Even from a distance the manor sitting astride the long hill across the valley had a brooding, sullen air. The gray stone pile and the square towers, the thick walls and battlements, the arched gates and surrounding walk, managed to convey a sense of challenge, of defiance, of daring any attempt to breach its sanctity, which—and if it does sound fanciful, it was nevertheless the impression imparted to me as I stared across at it from the top of the hill, and then as we began to descend into the valley—it might, deep down, have doubted its ability to resist. Sure, it had been there for centuries, since the days of the Tudor kings, yet there seemed to be a curiously temporary quality about it. Perhaps it was the country itself that created that illusion; it was so rolling and pleasant, so peaceful and green, so isolated, and quite different from anything I had known. Ravenswood Manor just didn't seem to belong there, and I was sure it wasn't like that with most of the other castles and mansions that dotted the British landscape, where I hadn't believed there was so much open space. Perhaps, too, it had been partly due to the fact that the sight had burst on me so suddenly. Although I had been expecting it, it had still come on me as a surprise.

A narrow river wound through the valley. Smooth green banks sloped up from either side of it. The running water was crystal-clear, and I could see the stones on the bed. It wasn't very deep. We crossed the river by a stone bridge, and then we were climbing again, through another stand of trees which blocked out the mansion. Then we were clear of the trees, and Ravenswood was above us, its crenellated turrets rising over the rim of the hill.

As we climbed still higher, the manor revealed itself in differing perspectives. It seemed to be revolving slowly against the vivid blue sky. The huge stone walls rose sheerly.

"What do you think?" James asked. "Impressive, what?"

"It looks quite gloomy," I observed as more of the massive structure came into view.

"It goes right back to Henry the Sixth and the Wars of the Roses. The Watmoughs have lived here since that time. They were local warlords, feudal barons. There they sat, in command of all they surveyed. Until now. Defeated at last by crippling taxes and death duties. Struck down by the killer welfare state. That was why it was necessary to get rid of the collection."

I quickly glanced at him. "I didn't realize it was *sold* to the Institute," I said.

"Oh, yes, sure. From what I gather, it was a long-standing arrangement. It wasn't a case of it going to the highest bidder. Sir Charles *wanted* the Barthelmy Institute to have it."

"What about the family? Didn't they raise any objections?"

"Not them." James laughed shortly. "Apart from the old girl, there's only Everard. All he seems to do is run up gambling debts. No, the money would have come in very handy."

The road turned sharply, and then we were at the top of the hill, with the great building looming above us. Despite the warmth of the sun, I felt a sudden chill. There was no warmth at all in those great gray walls. I stared up at the narrow embrasures, at the parapets, the entrance and the courtyard beyond, with a growing sense of foreboding. A shadow fell across me, and I felt quite cold.

From its eminence, Ravenswood Manor commanded a fine sweeping view of the surrounding countryside, the hills that rolled away on all sides, the neat green fields, the dark patches of forest, the tiny scattered villages and farmhouses, the lazily meandering river. James turned the car into a tree-lined avenue that led toward the manor wall. The avenue opened out into a broad sloping expanse of grass. James pulled the car up at the edge of the grass, next to the wall. Through the gateway I could see more of the courtyard and the stone steps leading up to a massive studded oak door. Beyond it were what looked like stables, now being used as garages, with a number of cars parked there.

A short distance away was another hill crowned with a thick stand of trees which ran down its flanks into the hollow between the two hills. From the wall a smooth expanse of green grass sloped down into the trees.

It was a relief to get out of the car. I stretched my cramped and aching muscles. The straining sound of the engine still echoed inside my head. I inhaled the fresh country air deep into my lungs. We were standing in the shadow of the mansion. The sunlight pricked the tops of the trees on the neighboring hill. It was very quiet.

"Well, here we are," James said.

"Yes, here we are."

"A home away from home." He pointed to the horizon that bounded the splendid unfolding vista below us. "Over there is Wales."

"It's beautiful country."

"Do you think you'll be all right?"

I laughed, a shade nervously. "I'll be fine."

He nodded toward the mansion. "The story goes that it's full of secret entrances and passageways, a precaution they took in those days when you never knew what was likely to bowl up on your doorstep. The collection is kept in one of the wings, away from the main part of the building. It's completely sealed off. A fortress within a fortress. It's the oldest part of the mansion."

"I had heard there was some security," I said.

"You'll see for yourself soon enough, I guess."

"I guess."

"And don't forget old Sir Mondrath." Suddenly he was serious. "You'll call me, won't you, if there's anything . . . ?"

"Yes, of course. But why do you keep saying that? Do you know something I don't?"

"Not really." He smiled. "No, nothing. Come on, let's go in." He reached into the car for my bag, then took my arm in a gesture that was quite spontaneous and pleasing. We began to walk toward the gate, the grass soft and springy beneath our feet.

We had walked only a few yards when, suddenly, the silence was shattered by the sound of splintering glass behind us. We swung toward the sound, just as the furious barking of dogs rose up somewhere within the reaches of the manor. James swore angrily under his breath.

We stared at the smashed rear window of the Mini. James let go my arm and walked quickly back to the car. I followed him. He stood with his hands on his hips, glaring into the car. "What the hell . . . ?"

There was glass all over the backseat and on the floor, and sitting in the middle of it was a golf ball. "Where . . . ? How . . . ?" He looked sharply around him.

"Hey there!" a deep voice boomed up from the hollow between the two hills. "Get that Tinker Toy out of the way and stand back. I'm playing through."

We stared at the woman who, with a golf bag on her shoulder, was brandishing a number-one club in her right hand as she came striding vigorously up the grassy slope toward us.

"Oh, my God," James groaned. "It's her ladyship herself."

7

Leaning on the golf club, Lady Watmough thoughtfully stroked her jaw and glared at the golf ball sitting on its bed of glass in the back of the car. "Now, that's a damned awkward play," she murmured. "But nothing ventured, nothing gained. I need to think." She swung away from the car and fixed first James and then me with a curiously fixed stare that took me some moments, already intimidated by her appearance, which, to say the least, was formidable, to realize was caused in part by the fact that she had one glass eye that was a different shade of blue from the good eye that blazed angrily at us from beneath the brim of the floppy tweed hat that sat on top of an unkempt crop of iron-gray hair. "Damn fool place to leave a car," she growled. "It spoiled my stroke." She was still glaring at me. "Who's this?" she demanded.

"This is Ali Baker," James told her. "From Chicago, the Barthelmy Institute."

"Yes, yes," Lady Watmough snapped impatiently. "Good appearance, but a bit delicate. Eh, girl?" She pronounced it "gel." "Do you play any sports at all?"

"A little tennis," I told her. "Swimming."

"Hunting, fishing, golf? No? Well, plenty of opportunity for that here. Plenty of fresh air. Good food. No place to bury yourself with musty old books."

She spoke quickly, her words clipped. She was a brusque, impatient woman, always, I suspected, on the move. Her impatience showed itself now in the way she viciously hacked at the grass with her golf club. She was a stocky woman with a heavy-jowled face that gave her a slightly bulldog appearance. Wispy strands of gray hair crept out from beneath the brim of her hat. She was wearing a gray hunting jacket with a fur collar, riding breeches, and brown boots. She glanced sourly once more into the car, shook her head, then, reaching in through

SECRET AT RAVENSWOOD

the shattered window, picked up the golf ball and dropped it into the pocket of her jacket. She hitched the golf bag on her shoulder, then, swinging her club, began to walk away. "Come on," she called over her shoulder. "Bring your bag. I'll take you to your quarters. You, too, young man. If you want a drink. Before you go. It's nearly teatime."

She strode away ahead of us. James looked at me, then with a shrug picked up my bag. "What about the window?" I asked him quietly.

"I don't know if I can master enough nerve to mention it. I think I'll send her a bill from London. It'll be safer."

We followed Lady Watmough beneath the wall to the gate. When she reached it, she turned and beckoned impatiently with the golf club. "Come on, you two," she called. "Don't hold back."

"Into the haunt of the Black Baron," James observed wryly. "He's probably watching us even now."

"Don't talk about it," I said half-seriously.

"Don't tell me you're nervous."

"All right. I won't tell you."

We moved in through the entrance into the chill shadow of the manor. It seemed to me we were moving back in time, sliding irresistibly into grim, bloody history. As the high, forbidding walls and towers closed in around us, there was the distinct feeling of being cut off from the rest of the world, and I could almost hear the distant chinking echo of chain mail, the snorting of horses, and the clash of steel on steel. I thought of the little that James had told me about the restless Black Baron, Sir Mondrath Watmough, and I felt even less well-oriented.

Above us, the sky was a small blue square. In some places the walls of the mansion were crumbling. In one of the walls was an iron trellis. Lady Watmough was waiting for us by the corner of the wall.

"Fixed a room for you in the old wing," she told me. Her immobile glass eye gleamed fanatically. "Over there."

I looked to where she was pointing, to the tower that rose at the far end of the courtyard. "That's where the collection is. You can work undisturbed."

The tower looked older and more sinister than the rest of the manor. Parts of its walls had crumbled, and great scars had been scored out of the black rock. There were gaping holes in the turret.

"It's the oldest part of the manor. It suffered quite heavy bombardment in the early days, but it's comfortable enough. The drafts are not too severe."

Staring up at the tower, I decided it didn't look comfortable at all. "The walls were never breached," Lady Watmough told me. "The

Watmoughs always held out. My heavens, this place has seen some history in its time—centuries of it. Always been a stronghold, and now, while the rest of the country's going to seed, we're still holding out. But for how long is anybody's guess. We all have to die sometime, and perhaps they will win in the end, what they started with their cannon, and then they'll take over, the rabble. Thank God I won't be here."

I exchanged a quick glance with James, who smiled and winked back at me. Lady Watmough abruptly changed tack. "How are you going to get all that stuff out of here?" she asked me, gesturing toward the old wing.

It was James who replied. "When she's done her check," he said, "she'll call me in London, and we'll arrange the packing and the shipment back to the States. She'll be with it all the way."

Lady Watmough studied me doubtfully. "Hummmmmph!" she snorted. "She looks very young, but I imagine they know what they're doing." She shook her head. "Those damn books. Charles lived only for them. It wasn't healthy. Now, at last, they're going to be useful for something."

She led the way across the courtyard to the stone steps that led up to the black-studded oak doors, one of which was slightly ajar. She pushed open the door and disappeared inside.

The hall was dark and cavernous, and lined on both sides by suits of armor that formed a sort of honor guard as we passed between them. The size of the place overpowered me, and I felt very small. Our footsteps echoed on the black-and-white-marble floor.

Lady Watmough eased the golf bag from her shoulder and propped it against the wall. "The other guests won't be back till later," she announced, and in that huge hall her voice echoed and reverberated, was carried up to the heavy beams that supported the high ceiling, and into dark corners. "They're out fishing or riding. Tomorrow's the hunt." She swung to face me, her good eye boring into me challengingly. "Do you like hunting, young lady?"

"I've never seen much point to it," I ventured.

She snorted derisively. "Backbone of the nation," she snapped. "In this country, hunting has always been equated with greatness. India, Africa, bagged 'em by the thousands, elephant, rhino, the Bengal tiger. Nothing namby-pamby about that." Mentally flinching beneath the relentlessness of her gaze, I felt she was accusing me of something, but I wasn't sure what. I couldn't think of a thing to say.

It was cold inside the hall, and as we passed between the suits of armor, I had the feeling I was being watched, appraised. A deep chill seemed to settle in the small of my back. I could feel it creeping along my bones.

At the end of the passage we came to a cham-

SECRET AT RAVENSWOOD

ber as large and as cavernous as the hall had been. A broad flight of stone steps swept upward. One wall was almost entirely taken up by a great fireplace. Above it, in a faded and peeling gilt frame, was the portrait of a fierce-looking man with wild dark eyes, a hooked nose, and a forked beard. The oils in which the portrait had been painted had cracked with age. The face was long and sallow, in vivid contrast to the rich waves of black shoulder-length hair that framed it. The bloodless lips were thin and cruel. But it was his eyes that were the most compelling feature; they blazed in the gloom of the chamber. They seemed to be seeking me out. I hesitated.

"The Black Baron himself," James told me in a hushed voice.

"Quite right," Lady Watmough said ahead of us. "He came out of the Welsh foothills with Owen Tudor and built this manor."

There were other portraits around the wall of the chamber, but none of them was as distinctive and compelling as that of Sir Mondrath Watmough. There was something about his features that drew and riveted my attention. I'm not sure what it was, but it was as if just beneath the surface of the painting, beneath the thick encrusted oils, there was a suppressed vitality striving for escape. I could almost see the fleeting changes of expression in those bold dark eyes. In a way I couldn't properly fathom, the painting disturbed me.

"Cold-looking fish, isn't he?" James observed in a whisper. Lady Watmough was climbing the steps and out of earshot.

"Yes, he is," I said with a barely repressed shudder. "Do you really think . . . ?"

"What?" he prompted when I paused.

I shook my head. "Nothing."

"Are you coming or not?" Lady Watmough called from halfway up the staircase.

With an effort I dragged my eyes away from the portrait and the eyes of the Black Baron, which now seemed to be mocking me.

8

The Black Baron's face was still imposed on my consciousness like a photographic negative as we followed Lady Watmough up the steps into another hall that stretched away ahead of us, and from which a number of passages had been cut into the rock. There were more portraits on the walls, early Watmoughs pinpointed in time by the costumes in which they were posed. There were Elizabethan Watmoughs, saturnine Cavalier Watmoughs, Georgian Watmoughs, and Victorian Watmoughs with muttonchop whiskers. As we walked past this illustrious cavalcade, I looked vainly around for another portrait of the Black Baron. But no, it seemed Sir Mondrath had been allotted his own special place in the hall below, away from these others. I wondered if there were any special reason for that.

The furniture was large and solid. There were carved chairs set at intervals around the walls, a gigantic table, a fireplace, and a marble mantelpiece. Arranged around the walls were a variety of ancient weapons, including pikes, lances, double-edged broadswords, arquebuses, crossbows, muskets, and flintlocks, and from a high gallery above one end of the hall hung faded and torn banners and standards worked in gold thread. It was a grim, formidable medieval place. I could feel the cold drafts swirling into the room through the passageways that opened from it.

At the end of the hall, Lady Watmough opened a door and led us into another, smaller room that was lighter and warmer and looked fractionally more comfortable.

The warmth came from a log fire that was roaring cheerfully in the fireplace, but even here I could feel the drafts of cold air. The furniture was solidly Victorian. Ranged around the fire were ottomans and deep armchairs complete with antimacassars, tasseled fringes, and footstools. There were polished black mahogany tables and sideboards with rows of copper plate and pewter that ruddily reflected the dancing flames of the fire. At one end of the room a narrow window looked out over the green hills and the shadows that were lengthening between them.

As we entered the room, a young man indolently unwound himself from the depths of one of the armchairs, and with his back to the fire studied us with an air of amused surprise. He nodded to James, then smiled loosely at me. James placed my bag down on the floor next to the door.

"This is the girl from America," Lady Watmough told the young man. "And you know young Montague, of course."

The young man was still watching me. "Of course. In fact, I was planning to come and see you when I'm up in town next. I thought a spot of lunch. There's something I'd like to discuss."

"You're bleeding that trust fund dry, Everard." Lady Watmough took off her soft tweed hat, and with a deft flick of her hand sent it spinning into one of the armchairs. "These are lean times. We have to pull our belts in a notch."

"Come now, Mother," Everard said languidly. "You know how the cost of living is rocketing skyward."

"And so are your gambling debts. What's the

matter? Are they putting pressure on you again?"

"For heaven's sake, Mother," he said with a touch of pain in his voice. "This is serious."

I suppose if one looked hard enough, a resemblance to Everard's distant ancestor, Sir Mondrath, could be detected. But it was as if, over the enormous number of years that separated them, Sir Mondrath's striking, bold features had been worn down into a bland smoothness. There was no defiance in Everard's dark, close-set eyes, only a lurking slyness; no cruelty in the thin mouth, only pettishness. It was a face that had no strength or real distinction. He was tall and his soft dark hair had been brushed carefully back over his ears. He was dressed casually but expensively in a blazer, cream slacks, and a high-necked maroon sweater. His shoes looked pure Gucci.

"Hasn't Harry Grahame been in touch with you?" James asked him.

"Yes, but surely it's only temporary, until they get things sorted out. And in the meantime..."

"It's out of our hands now, you see," James said simply.

"I don't believe that." Everard's face became tighter. "My credit has always been good. There has never been any question..."

James spread his hands in a gesture of helplessness. "You'd better take it up with Harry

Grahame," he said, looking a little embarrassed. "It's really Harry's pigeon." He shrugged. "We've had to tighten up all round, and the credit has been extended as far as it can go."

Everard gestured impatiently. His expression was petulant. I decided I didn't like him. "Oh, damn," he swore quietly, swinging away to face the fire with his hands behind his back.

"Sit down," Lady Watmough commanded. "By the fire. No time for business. Dammit, the hunt's on tomorrow. A snorter, Mr. Montague? I think I'll have one myself. Everard will fix us something. Miss Baker? You'll have a sherry?"

"A small one. Yes, please."

"There's whiskey if you prefer."

"Sherry will be fine."

Crossing to a sideboard, Everard opened one of the cupboards to reveal an array of bottles and glasses. He picked up a decanter.

"I'll have this one and go," James said when Everard had handed him his drink. "I've delivered Ali . . . Miss Baker safe and sound, and I should be off. If it's all right with you, Lady Watmough, I told Miss Baker I would pop around and see her tomorrow." He winked across at me. "See how she's getting on, and all that."

"If you like," Lady Watmough said with a shrug.

Having passed around the drinks, Everard had returned to the sideboard, where, leaning against it, he watched us speculatively and sipped his drink. Clearly there was something on his mind, and I guessed it had to do with money.

The armchair was comfortable, and I could feel the warmth of the fire against my legs. The logs sputtered, sparked, and shifted as the flames burned into them. A pile of logs stood on the hearth next to an ancient coal shuttle, a bellows, and a set of pokers. The fire was beginning to make me feel drowsy. I sipped the sherry. It was very smooth.

"I imagine you want to get down to work as soon as possible, young lady." From the armchair opposite, Lady Watmough studied me, the reflected firelight gleaming redly from her glass eye.

"Yes," I replied.

"There's a combination lock. I'll have to come with you. I'm the only one who knows what it is. Apart from the trustees. Charles took that precaution. He didn't trust anyone."

"The books are very valuable," I suggested.

"I don't know." She glared at me over the rim of her glass. "They might be worth a darn sight more as an insurance loss. Can't say the thought didn't cross my mind. But then there would be so many forms to fill in." She grimaced in disgust. "Leeches and bloodsuckers. They always find some loophole. Same with those damned legal people—eh, Montague?

SECRET AT RAVENSWOOD

Once they get their hooks in, they never let go. Mumbo-jumbo, thereafters, and parties of the first part, damn witch doctors in pinstripe trousers. All they do is confuse the issue. Isn't that right, Montague?"

"You're probably right, Lady W.," James said with a chuckle.

The flames flickered, and I was aware that Everard was watching me from across the room. His scrutiny made me feel awkward, but I tried not to show it. James finished his drink and stood up.

"Thanks for the drink," he said. "I'll be pushing off now."

Everard pushed himself away from the sideboard. "I'll show you out," he volunteered.

James's face clouded a little. Then it lifted, and he was smiling down at me. "I'll see you tomorrow, then. Keep some time free. All work and no play—that sort of thing."

He and Everard left the room. I could hear the voices receding in the hall outside, and I was left with a small feeling of disappointment. I wished he could have stayed a little longer. Through the window, the shadows were moving inexorably down the folds between the hills. Lady Watmough leaned forward from her chair and threw another log onto the fire, then, taking up one of the pokers, determinedly began to prod the burning wood, which sent up an angry flurry of sparks.

"A personable young man," she observed. "One of the Berkshire Montagues. Or is it Bedford? It doesn't matter. They're all so closely related." She looked shrewdly across at me. "He seems to have taken a shine to you, young lady."

"I don't know," I demurred, feeling the warmth creep up into my cheeks.

"Of course he has. I can tell. Just because I've only got one eye, it doesn't mean I can't see what's going on under my nose. All the signs are there, and when he said he was coming to see you tomorrow . . . It's too late to start working today," she said, abruptly changing the subject. "And tomorrow's Sunday. We'll be up at the crack of dawn, so I won't have a chance to take you to the library until later in the day. This will give you time to settle in."

Her tone brooked no argument, nor was it in my mind to offer any. My eyelids were becoming heavy. It was all beginning to catch up on me, and I was sure that nothing, not this grim mansion, the Black Baron, or anyone else would keep me awake. Lady Watmough was still poking the fire, and the sparks still flew. Pieces of charred wood crumbled beneath the jabbing tip of the poker. It was hard to believe there was any such thing as the Bokhara Commentary.

Replacing the poker in the rack, Lady Watmough heaved herself up out of the chair.

SECRET AT RAVENSWOOD

"Come on. I'll show you to your room. The others will be back soon."

Picking up my bag, I followed her out of the room into the great hall with the ancient weapons, battle standards, and the portraits of bygone Watmoughs. After the warmth of the fire, the drafts that swept down through the hall were quite icy. We turned down another passage that opened beneath the overhanging gallery. The walls of black stone seemed to close in on us on all sides. Our echoing footsteps rolled back around us. We came to a low flight of steps, and the narrow passage curved ahead of us, with other passages opening from it, so that I began to have the strange feeling that I was being led into a labyrinth that would eventually bring us back to the point from which we had started.

There were archways and still more passages. Steps wound down into the bowels of the manor. We came to the end of the passage, which was barred by a heavy grilled gate. Behind the gate, steps led steeply downward into the darkness. At right angles to the gate, another set of steps wound upward around the curve of the wall. Lady Watmough nodded to the gate.

"The cellars," she explained. "Once they were used as the dungeons. No one ever goes down there."

Beyond the grille, the walls gleamed faintly

in the thick gloom. I imagined I could hear the slow, steady sound of dripping water.

"The place is so vast," I said as we began to climb the steps away from the gate. "I wonder you're able to find your way around it."

"The upkeep is enormous," she remarked, "and servants are always a problem. Good ones are so hard to find."

The curving walls towered above us. "I've heard there's a ghost," I ventured.

"Rot and superstition!" she retorted. "It's what people expect. To have one on hand like some sort of mascot. These legends start back at a very early time. One has to be practical and treat them for what they really are."

Yet, looking around me as we came to the top of the steps and began to walk along another passage, I wasn't so sure. It was just the sort of dank, gloomy medieval place where such beliefs were likely to flourish like mushrooms. There was no room for practicality, because the place itself wasn't practical. It was a fantasy—a dark, brooding, gothic fantasy. It wasn't real, and there was nothing to which it could be equated in terms of present-day rationality. I was quite prepared to believe there was a ghost. In any event, Lady Watmough hadn't sounded at all convincing.

The cold crept upward through the uneven flags. At the end of the passage was a thick wooden door. "Here we are," Lady Watmough

SECRET AT RAVENSWOOD

announced, pushing down the heavy iron handle, and against its creaking protest, opening the door. "This is your room. It's close to the library, so it should be convenient enough for you."

I followed her into the room and put my bag down on the floor just inside the door. There was a key on the inside of the door. "As you can see, it's self-contained, so you have all the privacy you need. Now, if you'd like to unpack your things and freshen up a little, you can do that, then come back downstairs for a drink before dinner. Meet the others. If you want a bath, you'll have to let us know in advance. The hot water has to be brought up from downstairs." She nodded, and before I could say anything, she had left the room and closed the door behind her. I took a deep breath and looked around.

The room was furnished comfortably if a little sparsely. Next to the bed was a washstand bearing an enamel jug and basin. There were a wardrobe and a table. The closet-sized bathroom opened off the bedroom. The huge rust-stained bath occupied almost all the available space.

In the bedroom, a high narrow window looked out over the surrounding countryside. I moved across to it and looked out. The room was high up, and the view, undulating away to the distant hills and brought into sharp focus by the scoring shadows, was superb. It was like a patchwork quilt, with the river winding between the neat fields and the shadows lengthening among the stands of trees. It was very still. The room was on the other side of the manor from where we had approached it. The hill dropped sharply, in places almost precipitously, away beneath the retaining wall. A hedge-lined road cut across the countryside, and I guessed it was a continuation of the same road that we had turned away from at the neglected lodge to begin our climb up the hill. Looking across to my left, I could see part of the tree-covered hill adjoining the one on which the manor stood. I could see a portion of the grass slope that connected the two hills.

I was about to turn away from the window when I noticed a movement on the road at a point where it dipped in close to the escarpment. A car had emerged from the trees that sheltered that section of the road, and was moving slowly toward another, smaller stand of trees. It was a small black car, and was the only sign of movement I had seen in the minute or so I had been staring out the window. It disappeared into the trees, and for no particular reason I waited for it to come out and continue along the road at the foot of the hill.

But it didn't emerge from the trees. My curiosity mounting, I waited, but there was still no sign of it. It had stopped somewhere among the

SECRET AT RAVENSWOOD

trees, and I thought this was strange. Unless the car had broken down, there was, as far as I could see, no reason for it to stop there. There was no turnoff, no habitation.

Then, as I watched, I noticed another movement. Someone was walking down the grass slope toward the trees, a tall figure in a blazer and cream slacks, unmistakably Everard, walking quickly in the direction where the small dark car had stopped beneath the trees.

9

The other guests had returned by the time I came back downstairs into the room where the fire was still blazing merrily. Sitting or standing in various attitudes around the room, they looked up at me as I entered. The buzz of conversation momentarily faltered.

"Ah, here you are, my dear," Lady Watmough greeted me cheerfully. "You found your way down all right. Splendid. Just in time for a drink. This is the young lady I was telling you about," she announced to the room at large. "All the way from America."

"Come in and join the party." With a glass in his hand, Everard came toward me. His face was flushed, and he was a little unsteady on his feet. "After coming all this way, you *do* need a drink."

"Yes," Lady Watmough said. "Come in and meet everybody."

Apart from the Watmoughs, there were only a half-dozen people in the room. Everard handed me a glass of sherry as Lady Watmough performed the introductions.

There were colonel and Mrs. Cross, a tweedy couple who were definitely county. He had a ginger mustache and prominent front teeth, and she was wearing a double string of pearls. "Peter was in India for many years," Lady Watmough informed me.

"Forty years," Peter brayed. "Man and boy." He turned to his wife. "Eh, Mildred?"

"I do miss Simla," Mildred said mournfully.

"And I miss a damned good curry," her husband declared with a guffaw.

There was another couple called Willoughby, who didn't have much to say and kept very much to themselves. The remaining two guests were men. Rendal Griers was a tall, well-built man in his early forties, rather handsome with a high forehead and smiling dark eyes. Lady Watmough told me he had something to do with finance in the City, but she didn't know what exactly, as she didn't really understand such matters.

"Oh, come on, Florence.". Griers laughed. "You know more than you let on. She's really very shrewd," he said to me.

He had charm and polish, and he smiled a lot. He looked successful and assured. "All I know is that you're a fraud," Lady Watmough said good-humoredly. "A dabbler and a fraud. Any man who lives on his wits has to be suspect."

Griers's smile widened. "You know me too well."

We moved on to the last guest, who was standing by himself to one side of the fireplace, nursing a drink. "And here we have a countryman of yours. Isn't that right, Martin?"

"I guess so, ma'am," he replied. "But Los Angeles is a heck of a long way from Chicago. Of course, I know Chicago quite well."

"As you wish," Lady Watmough said. "Martin was a good friend of my husband's."

His name was Martin Keenan, and he was a sandy-haired rather insignificant man in his mid-forties. There was a light spattering of freckles across the bridge of a flat nose that looked as if it had been broken at some time, and his eyes were a very faded, washed-out blue. He sipped his drink awkwardly, as if he were a man not accustomed to strong drink.

SECRET AT RAVENSWOOD

Lady Watmough moved away, leaving us together. On the other side of the room, Everard was fixing himself another drink at the sideboard. Mildred Cross was fingering her pearls and looking hopeful.

"It sure is a weird feeling being in a place like this," Keenan said conversationally. "It's so huge and so cold. I don't know if I would ever get used to it. It takes a special kind of breeding, I guess."

"Lady Watmough said you were a friend of Sir Charles's," I said. I noticed his eyes were watchful. They kept darting around the room and didn't appear to miss a thing. I realized his appearance belied an inner alertness.

"Oh, yes, our paths crossed quite often. I'm over here in England on vacation, and when I got in touch with Lady Watmough, she kindly invited me up here for the weekend. It was very generous of her."

The Willoughbys were talking quietly to each other. Rendal Griers threw back his head and laughed at something someone had just said. Everard was leaning against the sideboard. He was drinking heavily.

From my window I had watched him disappear into the trees. Neither he nor the car had emerged from their shelter, and still puzzled, I had finally turned away from the window. It had been getting darker, and by the time I had left my room, after unpacking my bag and splashing some icy cold water onto my face, the lights had been turned on, pale and watery, but sufficient to enable me to make my way back to the main part of the manor.

Rather than dispel the shadows, the weak light had tended to consolidate them. I had walked quickly, nervously, pushing through the shadows that seemed to possess a watchful, living quality. I had hesitated by the iron grille Lady Watmough had told me led down to what had been the dungeons, and had the definite feeling there was something down there, a presence that was close to me but hidden by the shadows. I had felt a tingling sensation at the back of my neck. The lights had flickered, and I had hurried on down the passage. The lights had become stronger as I came out into the hall. I had moved quickly toward the low, welcoming sound of voices behind the living-room door. The first thing I had noticed was that Everard had already returned from his mysterious rendezvous among the trees.

The firelight was reflected from the walls and the heavy dark furniture. A pale ghostly moon had risen above the hills. "When you think of how much history there is in just this one place," Martin Keenan said, "it makes you think. It's awe-inspiring, although the plumbing could be better."

"I guess bad plumbing is part of the tradition," I observed.

He laughed. "You're probably right." His pale blue eyes were still watchful. "You have quite a handful with that collection," he said. "Sir Charles spent a great many years putting it together."

"Yes, I know," I said unenthusiastically.

There was a discreet tap on the door; then it opened, and a tall gray-haired, formally dressed man deferentially inclined his head and informed Lady Watmough that dinner was served.

"Thank you, Jakes," Lady Watmough boomed as the butler just as deferentially withdrew; then, clapping her hands together, she began to herd everyone out of the room. By the sideboard, Everard surreptitiously poured himself another generous whiskey.

To reach the dining room, we had to cross the hall beneath the disinterested gaze of the early Watmoughs and the ancient weapons and faded battle standards. The room opened beneath the gallery at the far end. Lady Watmough fussed around us like a mother hen.

We sat at a long table, with Lady Watmough at its head. I was placed next to Colonel Cross. The solid silver service reflected the fire that glowed comfortably in the fireplace. The food was served in covered silver platters. The main course was roast beef in thick, rich gravy, with fresh garden vegetables. I ate ravenously. I hadn't realized just how hungry I was. Colonel

Cross asked me if I had been to India, and I told him no, I hadn't.

"We lived so well there," he said regretfully. "There's never any point in going back. The changes have been so rapid. We could never adjust. It was the same coming back to England. The changes. Getting on in years, and it's not easy." He drank some claret and dabbed at his mouth with a napkin.

Martin Keenan sat quietly farther down the table. Near him, Everard brooded. Lady Watmough brought up the subject of revolution.

"Charles foresaw this happening . . . oh, more than twenty years ago, when we were there. Sirashar was such a pleasant city. The gardens were so green during the winter months, and now, with all these bombardments and riots, the gardens will be destroyed. They say the river is *choked* with bodies."

I was listening carefully. The name of the city had immediatcly conjured up the memory of Khamal and his seriousness in the London park. He had alluded to the revolution that was under way in his own country.

"They'll never destroy the oil wells," Rendal Griers supplied.

"They seem so very *sincere* about it all," Lady Watmough remarked wistfully.

"The story of Iran all over again," Colonel Cross said. "An exiled religious leader . . ."

Cutlery clinked against fine china. Glasses

SECRET AT RAVENSWOOD

were refilled. Griers leaned forward in his chair and smiled down the table at me. "I suppose you're quite familiar with the Bokhara Commentary, Miss Baker," he said.

The unexpectedness of the remark made me start. "Well, yes," I said slowly. "Familiar only in the sense that I have read about it." It could have been my imagination, but I sensed a subtle change in Martin Keenan's attitude. He seemed to be more intense somehow, more watchful. A silence had fallen over the table. Everybody was watching me, and I had the unnerving impression that I was being put through some form of examination.

"So what do you think?"

"About the Commentary?"

"Yes. Is it a hoax or not?"

"I don't know. I haven't really formed an opinion."

"Of course it's a hoax," Everard muttered from the other end of the table. "It's so much rubbish that's taken everyone in."

"Your father certainly didn't seem to think so," Lady Watmough snapped. "My God, when I think of all the trouble he went to to get the damned thing. Clandestine meetings and go-betweens, taxicabs and conferences in the dead of night. It was all very secretive. He had a bad stomach at the time, and a fever. We were in Baghdad, and it had to be smuggled across the border from Sirashar. I never saw the point of it myself, but then—who knows?—it meant something to him and those funny conspiratorial friends of his."

And to Khamal and *his* friends, I thought. Obviously the Commentary had been stolen from Sirashar, where, by a variety of devious routes, it had found its way from Bokhara, and ended up in the hands of Sir Charles Watmough. Now it was about to go to Chicago. Hoax or not—and that probably no longer mattered, such was the power to make anything believable, no matter how unlikely, the ability to transform fraud into truth by nurturing the mass sense of injury or righteousness—the fact remained that it was an object highly prized by someone, as it had been highly prized by Sir Charles Watmough, who had apparently gone to considerable lengths to acquire it. But why? The question formed itself in my mind. The argument that had raged about the document was an old one, so why was it suddenly important again? That it had a lot to do with the religious ferment that was taking place in Sirashar was evident.

"Frankly, I'll be glad to see the last of it," Lady Watmough declared. "I never felt easy having that thing in the place. There was something quite strange about the whole business."

Everard grunted, and pushing back his chair, lurched out of the room. The conversation drifted into other areas. Rendal Griers was relaxed and smiling again. I glanced across at him and wondered why he had so abruptly introduced the subject of the Bokhara Commentary. For dessert we were served sherry trifle topped with fresh cream.

I was feeling a little uneasy. For the time being, I had succeeded in pushing the Commentary right out of my mind, only to have it replaced by a preoccupation with the dark, gloomy, supposedly haunted manor which was to be my home for the next few days. Now it had been thrust back to the forefront, together with the memory of Khamal's veiled threat that his approach to me was by no means his last resort. My appetite gone, I listlessly spooned my dessert. Colonel Cross had embarked upon a long, involved, and to judge by the expressions of the others, patently boring story, accompanied by a number of high-pitched titters which made his mustache move around a bit, about a maharajah and his model-train set. The Willoughbys smiled vapidly. She was rather large, and her name was Geraldine. He had something to do with agriculture. Rendal Griers drummed his fingers on the white damask tablecloth. Lady Watmough's glass eye was red and wicked. The plates were quietly taken away.

After dinner we drifted back out to the drawing room for coffee and brandy. Everard wasn't there, and shortly afterward, pleading tiredness, Martin Keenan excused himself. Rendal Griers stood with his back to the fire, holding his cup and saucer.

"I do like to come up here," he told me. "Poke around a bit, explore. There's always something new to find. I have a thing about old mansions. The atmosphere, the sense of history—it makes you think. I've been coming up here for some years now, and I'm still intrigued." When he smiled, dimples appeared in his cheeks.

Sitting beside the fire, I began to feel drowsy. My eyelids became heavier, and the voices around me took on a hollow, disembodied quality. The moonlight washed against the windowpane. I stifled a yawn.

". . . best damn curries anywhere in the East," I heard the colonel say. I dragged myself up out of the armchair.

"I think I'll go up to my room now," I told Lady Watmough. "I am rather tired."

The glass eye glinted. "As you wish. Will you be able to find your way? I could ask Jakes to go with you."

"No, no, I'll be all right."

I said good night to the others and left the room. Outside, the chill was bitter and complete. I hurried across the hall, and had the feeling that the eyes of the Watmough ancestors were following me. Then, in the feeble light,

SECRET AT RAVENSWOOD

there was the long walk between the black, enclosing walls, through the archways, and up the steps. The farther I walked, the smaller and more completely alone I felt. Alone? No, that wasn't quite right. There was once more the disturbing sense of a presence not very far away, that I was being watched. The shadows stirred slightly around me, and once I thought I heard a soft scraping sound behind me. I stopped, and with my heart beating faster, swung back to face the way I had come, and peered into the gloom. But I saw nothing, only the shadows and the gleaming black walls. I moved even more quickly along the passage until I was almost running. I came to the grilled gate and stopped again. I thought I had heard another sound, but as I listened, every nerve of my body strained, all I could hear was the steady thumping of my heart. I stared through the grille into the impenetrable darkness at the foot of the steps. By this time my overworked imagination was playing tricks on me, and I thought I saw a slight movement in the shadows beyond the gate. I ran up the curving steps and along the passage to my room. Closing the door behind me, I turned the key in the lock. I leaned against the door, my heart still pumping furiously. I was frightened, and I didn't know why. I listened intently, but I heard nothing outside the room. All the same, it took some moments before the pumping of my heart subsided.

The moonlight fell across the bedcover. I moved across to the window and looked out. Everything was silver and black, and very, very still. It was a landscape that was quite ghostly. The stars were out. I began to prepare myself for bed.

Huddled under the blankets, I allowed myself to slowly relax. I began to drift....

Then, suddenly, I was wide-awake, and my heart was beating rapidly again. I had been asleep, and something had awoken me. The furniture stood solidly black in the moonlight that streamed in through the window. Then I heard it, the slow, heavy sound of dragging footsteps in the passage outside. I could hardly breathe. I couldn't move, although the impulse was there to shout, to run, fling open the door to confront whoever it was out there. I lay there clutching the blankets to my chin, listening to the dragging footsteps as they drew closer to my door. It was as if I were trapped by the paralyzing grip of my fear. The footsteps stopped, and through the door I could hear the sound of heavy breathing.

Then, as I watched, the door handle began to move. I could only just stifle the urge to scream as I stared in helpless fascination at the downward-turning handle. It stopped moving, and then I heard the most chilling sound of laughter, soft yet maniacal, echoing between the stone walls as the heavy dragging footsteps began to move away from the door and back along the passage.

10

Although it came from some distance away, the ragged sound of the horn was loud enough to jolt me into full, startled wakefulness. I heard it again, and knew I hadn't been dreaming. I heard dogs barking noisily, and people shouting. The sounds were filtered up to my room from somewhere far below; then, as the horn sounded yet again, I remembered the hunt.

The room was full of gray light, which gradually grew brighter. It was going to be another fine day. I lay in the bed listening to the sounds that came up from below—from the courtyard, I guessed—as the memory of what had happened during the night came flooding back.

It could have been a mistake, I thought, someone who had taken the wrong turning—such an easy thing to do in this place—had tried the wrong door, then, realizing the mistake, had gone away. If I could convince myself of that, I would feel much easier. But I couldn't feel easy, couldn't convince myself that the explanation was as simple or convenient as that. The more I thought about those dragging footsteps, the heavy breathing on the other side of the door, and then the laughter that had sounded so unearthly, the more inescapable was the conclusion that someone had deliberately tried to get into my room. I had had the foresight to turn the key in the lock, but if I hadn't . . . The thought was frightening.

I hadn't been able to sleep. I had stared up at the changing patterns of moonlight on the ceiling and walls, trying hard to still my racing, tumultuous thoughts and force on them some sort of order. There had to be an answer, but I didn't know how to go about finding it. I had been frightened. I had felt so terribly alone, and my one dominating thought was to get away from Ravenswood and the evil I was beginning to think permeated its thick walls. I had told myself I would probably think differently in the morning, and finally I had calmed sufficiently to drift into a tossing, restless sleep, to be abruptly woken again by the hunting horn.

Pushing back the blankets, I swung my feet onto the cold floor and moved across to the window. The hills were tipped with sunlight. The river sparkled, and puffy white clouds floated across the pale blue sky. The early-morning dew glistened on the grass and on the leaves of the trees. I decided it would be nice to go for a walk.

The barking of the dogs grew louder, and then I saw them, running down the slope away from the manor, fanning out as they neared the bottom. Hard on their trail came the riders, about a dozen of them, in red hunting jackets and peaked caps, urging their mounts faster so that they were riding hell for leather. I watched them spreading out across the countryside, leaping over hedges and fences until they were out of sight over the crest of a low hill. It was a fine morning for a hunt.

About half an hour later, after I had washed and dressed, I gingerly unlocked the door of my room, and easing it open, wincing at the loud creaking noise it made, glanced nervously out into the passage. My nerves were still not completely settled, and I didn't know what might be out there. The passage was empty. Moving out into it, I closed the door behind me.

SECRET AT RAVENSWOOD

Even in daylight there was still the same daunting sense of oppression as I made my way along the passage and down the steps. I moved quickly past the gate that led down into the cellars, and along the passage away from it. It was invariably there, by the gate, that I had the feeling I was close to a living, watching presence.

The manor seemed deserted. I didn't hear a sound, and the silence was quite eerie. I walked as quietly as I could so as not to disturb the silence. Even when I came to the hall, I heard nothing. I might have been alone in the manor, and that thought didn't appeal to me at all. The faces in the dusty portraits were devoid of life and expression.

Only Sir Mondrath's face showed any sign of expression. At the foot of the steps I stopped and stared at the portrait, as if my eyes had been drawn to it against their will. Perhaps it was the positioning of the light, or the angle from which I was studying it, but it seemed to me that his expression had undergone a subtle change. There was a knowingness about it, an air of complicity. I moved deeper into the hall and looked at it again. The expression was still there. I walked quickly past the suits of armor that lined the entrance hall to the front door.

It wasn't until I was outside that I realized how musty the air inside the manor had been. The air outside was clear and biting, almost intoxicating. I took a number of deep breaths, and felt momentarily dizzy. I began to walk across the courtyard toward the gate. The silence persisted.

Then I was on the grass, and the sun was shining pleasantly down on me, which made me feel better and dispersed even more my fears of the previous night. I began to walk down the slope toward the neighboring hill. I was almost prepared to believe that the attempt to enter my room had been a mistake after all. And the laughter? . . . It mightn't have been laughter at all. It could have been someone coughing, for instance.

The dew still coated the grass, and my feet left tracks across it. The wall of the manor loomed above me to my right, and then I was away from it, approaching the trees. I thought of James, and wondered if I should have waited for him before starting out on my walk. But it was much too early. He hadn't told me what time he intended coming to Ravenswood, but I assumed it would be later in the morning, perhaps early afternoon. I was looking forward to seeing him again. I had already made up my mind to tell him of my fears as I had lain in my bed and listened to the dragging footsteps in the passage outside. Of course, he would laugh and tell me it was no one less than the Black Baron himself abroad on one of his nocturnal perambulations. The Black Baron. . . . I

SECRET AT RAVENSWOOD

walked faster. I had almost reached the trees. Was it possible? *Was* there such a thing as a ghost? The sun was strengthening all the time, and everything was so fresh and sweet-smelling. I was walking in the English countryside. Of course, it wasn't possible. The manor had been weaving a sinister sort of spell on me, and for the moment at least, I was free of it.

I reached the hollow between the two hills, and followed it as it dropped down into the trees. The hills rose on either side of me. Now that I was away from the manor, I walked more slowly. I felt hungry. Nobody had said anything about breakfast, and I assumed that the hunting party would be breakfasting when they returned to the manor. When, probably depended on how long it took them to catch up with the fox. I could feel the sun's warmth against the back of my neck.

I wandered aimlessly among the trees. The fallen leaves crunched soggily beneath my feet. Moisture dripped from the overhanging branches. The trees thinned out, and I found myself on the grassy bank of the river. Ravenswood was out of sight over the hill that ranged away above me. Birds were singing, and the clear water gurgled over the stones on the riverbed, forming eddies as it cascaded thinly through the narrow passages in the rock. I could see the stone bridge farther along the bank where it curved to follow the river. I began to walk toward it. I felt much better, much more relaxed. But I knew I would eventually have to return to the manor. I still had work to do.

As I walked beside it, the river became deeper. Once I saw something large and silvery darting beneath a ledge of rock. I reached the bridge, and crossing it to the opposite bank, continued along it in the same direction. The sound of the running, trickling water was soothing. The bank sloped gently up to the trees. I walked on around the curve of the river, following the base of the hill. The river turned away from the hill and meandered across the country between the distant fields and meadows. I kept following the base of the hill.

Unaccountably, I found myself thinking about Milly Fellowes. It had been a rainy night when the car had struck her. She had been working late in the library, as she often did, and was on her way back to her apartment. I realized now how much I missed her. She had been very patient with me when I had started work at the Institute. My mistakes had been taken for granted, and gradually some of her enthusiasm had rubbed itself off onto me. *She* would not have been deterred by the intimidating ambiance of Ravenswood Manor, and would have given the Black Baron short shrift if she had encountered him. She had been exceptionally single-minded. She certainly

SECRET AT RAVENSWOOD

wouldn't have listened to Khamal's offer, let alone even consider it. I stopped walking. Khamal had intimated to me that evening in the park that an approach had been made to someone else to secure the Bokhara Commentary. I remembered him saying that a similar stubbornness had been encountered. I tried to comprehend what he had meant by this. Was it possible that that approach had been made to Milly, and she hadn't listened? Then, on the eve of her departure, the accident, a car that hadn't stopped, a hit-run driver. Were they in some way connected? If they were—and there was nothing to say they were—then the significance was frightening, or could be frightening. I didn't know what to think. No, I told myself, it had to be a coincidence, or perhaps I was merely comforting myself by taking the easy way out. In the meantime, the sun was shining, the birds were singing, people were out hunting innocent foxes, and I had work to do. I certainly didn't think I would ever see Khamal again. He had made me a proposition, and I had turned him down; it was as simple as that. Milly's death had been an accident, and that was all. These things happened all the time. All the same, I couldn't help wondering.

I worked my way around the foot of the hill. Ahead of me, running across the foot of the hill, was a tree-lined bank. I headed toward it, across a patch of smooth green grass. I climbed the bank and moved into the shadow of the trees. I thought it was time to start making my way back to the manor. The sunlight, slanting down through the trees, formed golden pools on the carpet of falling leaves. I came to another bank, and scrambled up it.

I was standing beside the road. It was very quiet. I looked up and down the road, not sure at first which way to turn, and then saw, about a hundred yards along to my right, the old crumbling lodge at the turnoff that led up the hill to Ravenswood. I began to walk toward it, keeping to the grass at the side of the road. The walk and the fresh air had whetted my appetite.

Reaching the lodge with its broken shutters and with half the tiles on its roof missing, I cut in behind it, preparing to climb the hill where it was not so steep, and moving diagonally away from the road. Ahead of me I noticed something glinting among the trees a short distance from the lodge. Curious, I moved toward it, staring through the trees in an attempt to identify the metallic object from which the sun had momentarily glinted. Then, as I came still closer to it, I saw it was a car that had been parked off the road in a clearing among the trees. It was a small dark car of the same make I had observed from my room in the manor the evening before. The tracks it had made as it was driven off the road across the grass and

SECRET AT RAVENSWOOD

fallen leaves looked comparatively fresh. There was no one near the car, and the thought crossed my mind that it might have been abandoned. I stopped again, and listened, but I heard nothing but the birds in the trees. I moved across to the car and peered in through the closed windows.

The first thing I noticed was a dark glistening patch on the front seat, and some smears on the steering wheel. I backed away from the car, and then I noticed that the leaves around my feet had been disturbed, as if something heavy had been dragged through them. I saw a tiny drop of red clinging to a solitary blade of grass, then more drops sparkling in the sun. I stared wildly around me. Something was very wrong. It looked as though a struggle had taken place, and the red smears that lay across the grass and leaves were unmistakably blood. I backed farther away from the car. There was more blood on the ground. The leaves had been churned violently.

The trail led away from the car into the trees. Reluctantly, fearing what I might find, I followed it, pushing my way through the heavy thickets, some of the smaller branches of which had been snapped. Other branches reached out and plucked at my sweater. The trail seemed to be leading back to the disused lodge at the fork of the road. I could see its broken walls through the trees in front of me.

I was approaching the lodge from the rear. Beyond it was the lane that climbed the hill toward Ravenswood. The leaves crunched softly beneath my feet, and although I was walking as quietly as I could, it seemed I was making an awful lot of noise.

There was blood, there was danger, and suddenly I felt cold. The lodge was just ahead of me. Listening, I edged around the wall to the door. I came to a window with a broken shutter hanging lopsidedly from the frame. Reaching up, I looked in through the opening, but saw nothing apart from bare floorboards, a wall, a broken chair. I lowered myself and moved around to the door.

The door was ajar. Tentatively I placed my hand against it and held my breath until there was a pain in my chest and I was forced to let it go as the door slowly and ominously, with a creaking of its rusted hinges, swung inward. I peered into the dim room as it was gradually revealed to me, but still saw nothing. Still fighting against my overriding instinct to run, I stepped into the room.

There was dust everywhere, and thick cobwebs in the corners of the low ceiling. The windows were broken, and there were cigarette butts and empty beer bottles, blankets and old newspapers scattered across the floor, as if someone had camped here once. There was another door. Slowly, carefully, I moved across to it. It was still not too late, I told myself. I had looked into the lodge, and that was enough. I could turn back now and assure myself that I had done all I could to satisfy my curiosity. But I hadn't. I *knew* I hadn't. There was that other door. I could smell something now—something sweet and cloying, a sickly aroma. My heart was pounding fiercely, and I was very frightened. Not too late, a voice shrilled inside my head. Turn back. Turn back now.

I pushed the door open, and gasped. There, propped in a sitting position against the far wall, was a man, his eyes staring hugely, his lips twisted back from strong white teeth in an unearthly grimace. At first I thought he was wearing a red shirt and that there was a thin red kerchief around his neck. Then I made out the deep gash in his throat, and realized that his shirt was drenched with blood. With all the color drained from his face, Jamil was very dead.

Quickly I backed out of the room; then, not caring how much noise I made, I ran through the other room to the door. I ran outside. Behind me, a twig snapped.

11

I plunged through the trees and thickets, not knowing, not caring where I was heading. All I knew was that I had heard a sound behind me, and I had panicked. The branches seemed to be trying to restrain me as I pushed through the thickets. I was running as fast as I could, sure that I was being followed, but too frightened to look back to see how much my pursuer was gaining on me. I was certain I could hear the crashing in the undergrowth behind me, and at any moment expected a hand to reach out and grab me, fling me onto the ground. My desperation spurred me.

There had been someone outside the lodge. Of that I was certain. The snap of the twig had been so loud, so distinct, and had come from the thick bushes behind the lodge. It had all happened so quickly—the abandoned car, the trail of blood, and Jamil's grotesquely grinning corpse propped up against the wall, his throat sliced almost from ear to ear. There had been the shock of the discovery; then, when I had backed out of the lodge, the snapping twig. It had sounded like a shot.

I was running away from the road, down the hill through the trees, carried forward by the rush of my momentum. I kept seeing Jamil's face. He had been murdered—that was all I was able to absorb. That and the fact that his murderer had been waiting outside, was now chasing me through the trees....

The trees thinned, and I was sprinting along the top of a high bank that sloped steeply down to the river. There were more trees in front of me. Suddenly my foot caught in a root, and with a wrenching, twisting pain in my ankle I was flung heavily to the ground. I scrambled up onto my knees. My breath was coming now in great wet sobs. A sharp pain shot up my leg from my twisted ankle. I brought myself up onto my feet and started forward again, easing as much as I could the pressure on my wrenched ankle. The pain wasn't too bad. I could still manage.

Then once more I was rushing down through the trees, sliding on the grass, and flailing my arms in a desperate attempt to keep my balance. The undergrowth caught my feet and tried to trap me. Branches whipped back at me. I was struggling for breath.

The river was just ahead of me. I had lost all sense of direction. Once again the trees were behind me, and I was out in the open. Too late I realized I should have remained among the trees, where I would have had a better chance of eluding my pursuer.

My pursuer.... For the first time since the snapping twig had triggered off an instant and unthinking response, I experienced a shadowy doubt that I *was* being pursued. Still running along the bank above the river, I ventured a quick glance over my shoulder. There was no one on the grass behind me. I stopped and looked up at the trees above me, but still saw nothing. It still didn't mean I was safe, however, that I had somehow managed to shake him off. He could have easily been up there in the trees, watching me and preparing to head me off as I tried to get back to Ravenswood.

It was so quiet and peaceful that it was difficult to believe that Jamil was sitting up in the deserted lodge with his throat cut; that I had been so gripped by fear that for those few hec-

SECRET AT RAVENSWOOD

tic, blundering minutes my only impulse had been to escape an unknown pursuer I was certain intended to kill me. Beside me, on the riverbed, weeds waved gently with the motion of the clear, flowing water. In the distance I could hear dogs barking. It was warm in the sun. Still apprehensive, expecting anything at all to happen, I began to walk along the riverbank. I kept glancing up into the trees, and still saw nothing. Although I kept close to the bank, I could still be seen from the trees. As I walked, I tried to sort things out in my mind.

There *had* been someone outside the lodge. Whatever else I had thought in the course of my headlong rush, I knew I had not imagined the sound of the snapping twig. It could have been an animal, of course, but somehow I didn't think so. I was sure I would have heard a startled animal running off into the undergrowth, despite my panic. But the important thing was that Jamil was dead, murdered, and I had to tell someone. I was heading back toward Ravenswood. I could see the stone bridge gradually appearing around the bend in the river, and the tall hill beyond which stood the manor. I had to tell someone about the body in the lodge. There would be questions, and if I were asked if I had seen the man before, I would have to admit I had.

There were other questions that needed to be answered. For instance, what was Jamil doing near Ravenswood? I thought I had seen him in Bridgnorth while James and I were having lunch in the pub, driving a small dark car. Later, from my room in the manor, I had seen a similar car stop among the trees, then, a short time afterward, Everard Watmough striding down the grass slope toward where it had disappeared. The next time I had seen the car, it had been parked off the road near the old crumbling lodge. Inside the lodge I had found Jamil's body. It had been the same car; it couldn't have been just a coincidence. I had seen Everard walking toward the car. That connection having been established, did that mean Everard had killed him? Jamil hadn't been long dead when I found him; the blood had still been fresh.

I was about halfway across the bridge when I heard the sound of an engine behind me. A car was coming down the road to the bridge. I glanced quickly around, but the car was behind a bend in the road, and I couldn't see it. Experiencing by now a familiar spurt of panic, and believing I was in danger again, I looked desperately around me for a place to hide, but I was in the middle of the bridge, and there was open ground at either end. I pressed back against the low stone wall of the bridge and stared toward the sound of the car as it approached the bend. I didn't even have a chance to run to the end of the bridge, where I could have hidden myself on the bank beneath it.

Then the car came into view, and a huge surge of relief swept over me. It was a small red, mud-stained, boxlike Mini Minor with a shattered rear window. I saw James's familiar figure behind the wheel. Pushing myself away from the wall, not knowing whether to laugh or cry, I began to run toward the car. I didn't care anymore. I didn't know I could be so happy to see him.

Seeing me, he stopped the car at the end of the bridge and put his head out the open window.

"Hey," he called. "Why the rush? I must say I didn't expect such a big welcome."

By the time I reached the car, I was out of breath again. "Thank God!" I cried. "I didn't know it was you. I thought . . ."

His smile faded, to be quickly replaced by an expression of concern. "What's the matter, Ali? You look flustered." He opened the door and stepped out onto the road. He was wearing faded jeans and an old green sweater.

Quickly, breathlessly, I blurted it out. His face was expressionless as he listened to me. I tried not to leave anything out. I told him about the car, and the signs of something having been dragged through the leaves. I told him how I had found Jamil's body inside the lodge, how somebody had been in the bushes outside, and how I had run, panic-stricken, in the belief that he was chasing me. I told him about the proposition Khamal had put to me in Kensington Gardens, and how Jamil had hovered watchfully in the background.

"Well, we'd better go and take a look," he said when I had finished. He moved around the car and opened the passenger's door. "Here, hop in. It won't take a moment. Then we'd better call the police." When I hesitated, he looked at me over the top of the car and smiled reassuringly. "No need to worry. You can stay in the car. No sense in going through all that again. It must have been pretty gory."

"It was," I fervently assured him.

After James had reversed the car onto the grass at the side of the road, we drove back up the hill. As we climbed, the towers of Ravenswood Manor came into view and seemed to rise with us. James was hunched forward over the wheel, an intense expression on his face. We came to the top of the hill, and then we were descending through the trees.

"So you think this is somehow bound up with the Bokhara Commentary," he said at last.

"It's the only connection I'm able to make."

He nodded. "Seems there's something strange going on. I wonder what Everard's part is in all this. The murderer? No, I don't think so. He's a most unlikely murderer, I must say. I could never see him slitting anyone's throat.

Poison perhaps, but not cold-blooded throat-slitting. It's not his style, and I'm a fairly good judge of character." He chuckled softly as he negotiated the car around a sharp bend. "Poor Everard. He really is quite desperate, you know. He needs money, and quite a lot of it—and there just isn't any more. It's been used up, and he's been living on credit for some time now, and with the economic climate the way it is, the investments are steadily going bad. He doesn't seem to understand this. His gambling debts are high, and now the heavies are after him. What can he do?"

It was starting to fit together. Of course. It was obvious. If he needed money so badly, and Khamal needed the Bokhara Commentary so badly, and if an approach had been made to Everard in much the same way as an approach had been made to me, then that established a connection between Everard and Jamil, who had very likely been acting as a go-between.

"Are you thinking what I'm thinking?" James asked.

"What's that?"

"Everard needs money. Here is a way for him to get it—if he can produce the Bokhara Commentary and pass it on to your friend . . . what's his name again?"

"Khamal."

"Yes, but it's hardly likely that he will kill the goose that lays the golden egg. Unless, of course, he has already managed to pass it on, and now he's covering his traces. But again, that's hardly likely. It's not in his character."

"Is it possible he could have gotten hold of the commentary?" I asked.

"Hard to say, but I doubt it. You heard what Lady Watmough had to say about it yesterday. But if he were determined enough . . . Well, perhaps. But I don't really think so."

We reached the bottom of the hill and turned in off the road at the other side of the lodge. "Wait here," James said, opening the door and stepping out onto the grass. "Won't be a minute."

I watched him walking through the trees, shouldering his way through the thickets as he moved around behind the lodge. Now that I was alone again, I felt nervous. I silently wished him to hurry back. I looked around at the trees, but everything was still. Perhaps, I thought in my rising imagination, everything was *too* still. Then I saw a movement among the trees, and tensed instinctively. But it was James returning from the lodge, and I relaxed.

"Ali, come here." He was beckoning to me.

Doubtfully, and reluctant to see the body in the lodge again, I climbed out of the car and walked across the grass to where he was waiting for me with a puzzled expression.

"Ali, are you sure this is the place?"

SECRET AT RAVENSWOOD

It was my turn to be puzzled. "Yes, I am. Why? He's inside."

"Well, you'd better come and take a look," he said quietly.

We walked back into the trees and around the side of the lodge to the entrance. The door was still open. We moved into the lodge. The cobwebs were still there, undisturbed, as were the signs of an earlier occupation. I pointed to the inner door. "In there," I said in a whisper.

James strode across to the door. When he reached it, he stopped and nodded back to me. "Come."

I moved slowly, warily, across to him, my confusion mounting. He stepped to one side, and I looked into the room.

The room was empty. There was nothing. Jamil's body had gone.

"But . . ." I gasped. "I don't understand. He *was* there." I looked around for a sign that would confirm this, but there was nothing. There wasn't even a drop of blood. "The car . . . outside . . . through the trees." I pulled away from the door. "I'll show you."

I was almost running through the trees to where the car had been partially concealed from the road. I came to the clearing and stopped abruptly. The car was gone.

12

"I don't understand it," I said weakly. "He *was* there. I wasn't imagining it."

With his fingers hooked into the pockets of his jeans, James moved around the clearing, kicking idly at the leaves. "Whoever it was," he murmured, "he went to a lot of trouble to cover his tracks. And he didn't have much time to do it in."

I walked across to him. "You don't think I made it all up, do you?"

He looked up at me and slowly shook his

head. "There was somebody here. There's no doubt about it. These leaves have been freshly turned, and look over there." He pointed down to the leaves. "That looks like blood to me."

I stared down at the faint rusty smear across the leaf he was indicating. "What do we do now?" I asked.

"This car—what make was it, do you know?"

"No, I don't."

"I was wondering . . . There was a small Escort. It nearly ran me off the road, but I didn't think any more about it—until now. There was no reason to make any connection. But now . . . It was probably the same car. Dark, you say? Dark green?"

"Yes," I told him.

James looked pleased with himself. "Then it *must* have been the same car. I didn't see who was driving. The sun was in my eyes . . . there was a bend in the road, and I didn't see him until the last moment . . . had to swerve. He was driving very fast." He took his hands out of his pockets and sighed. "He must have been here all the time, watching you, and then, when he saw you had found the body, he knew he had to move it. He would have had to move the car anyway, and the chances are that the body would have been in the lodge for some time before it was discovered, possibly by some tramp who might decide to camp there. There was certainly no guarantee it *wouldn't* be discovered." He talked quietly but fervently. I felt much better now that he was with me, that he was able to treat the matter so calmly. After all, it was a dead man I had discovered. I was still shaken. "No, what I really think is that the body wasn't meant to stay there. It would have been moved, when there was more time to do it. Which might seem to suggest that the murderer was working against time and that he intended to return later to dispose of the *corpus delicti* when he had more time to do it." He smiled at me. "How's the reasoning so far?"

"Fine—you're doing just fine." I smiled back at him, touched by the infectiousness of his own.

"See? You're feeling much better already." He reached out, and his hand gently cupped my chin, raising my face toward his own. "It must have been quite a shock for you."

Our faces were so close, James's presence so immediate and concentrated, that I almost cried out and flung myself against him, to be enfolded in his arms, drawn against him. Abruptly I turned my head away. James dropped his hand and looked abashed. "Oh, I say, I'm awfully sorry. I shouldn't have done that."

"No, it's not that," I said quickly, smiling up at him again. "I was just thinking that if he— the murderer—was here all the time, he knows I have seen the body."

"The late lamented," James said. "That's why there had to be a hurried change of plans. Instead of waiting, he had to get the body and the car out of there as soon as possible. You didn't see who it was, and we don't know where the body is." He took my arm and began to lead me back through the trees to the car. "What do we do now? Well, the first thing is to inform the police, and the nearest station is at Bridgnorth. But without the body . . ." He shrugged. "They might listen to me, and they'll want to ask you some questions. But leave it to me. I'll take you back to Ravenswood." We stopped among the trees, and he was looking at me intently. "You will be careful, won't you?" he said earnestly. "You will keep your eyes open and be careful?"

Emotion was welling up in me. His eyes were gazing fondly into mine, and I didn't know what was happening. I felt quite helpless. The sunlight glanced sharply through the canopy of leaves above us. Something was happening to me, something it seemed had been foreordained, and I was quite powerless to resist it. For the moment I had forgotten about the manor, and the body I had found in the deserted lodge, the Bokhara Commentary, and everything else. There was only the moment, this sweet, delicious, inevitable moment as James drew me into his arms and our lips met. There was no need to speak; there was nothing for either of us to say. The sun moved slowly above the trees, and for me, in that moment, there was no such thing as fear, or anything but the heightened rush of feeling that enveloped me.

As we drove back up the hill away from the lodge, I said, "It could have been Everard."

"It could have been anyone. Somebody from the manor." James chuckled. "Why, it could even have been me."

I looked at him sharply. "It wasn't, was it?"

"Of course not." He took one hand from the steering wheel and placed it on my thigh. "Surely you don't believe that."

"Perhaps it's just that I'm not in the mood for jokes," I replied. "I'm not looking forward to going back."

He lifted his hand from my thigh. "You don't have to go back, you know."

"I must. Oh, I'll be all right. Everything happened so fast, and I haven't had a chance to settle in. And the place itself, the mansion—it's so strange. Last night . . ." I hesitated, then, when he glanced at me expectantly, went on. "Someone tried to get into my room. I heard footsteps, very heavy, then someone laughing."

"Not the Black Baron," he suggested lightly.

"I knew you would say that," I retorted, irritated by his flippancy. "Really, I hardly think this is the time—"

"I'm sorry," James broke in hastily. "But it

SECRET AT RAVENSWOOD

could have been a mistake, the wrong door. Who do you think it could have been?"

"I've no idea."

"It seems to me a lot of strange things are going on in that place," he observed.

We drove on a short distance in silence. We were almost at the top of the hill. James began to whistle softly. "You know," he said, "I think I'm in love. Does that amaze you?"

I smiled. "You're very quick to make up your mind."

"In that place, surrounded by menace, where a *murder* had just taken place. Isn't it marvelous? Those things didn't seem to matter anymore. They didn't really concern us. Did you feel the same way?"

"It was very quiet," I said. "For those few moments . . . so peaceful. I guess . . . well, you'll have to let me think." The words tumbled out and became caught up with each other. I was more than conscious of my awkwardness, of the color rising in my cheeks. I was confused, and didn't know what to say. It was too soon. Everything was happening so quickly.

"All the time you need," he said. "We don't need to rush things. There's plenty of time."

I remained silent. We came to the top of the hill, and there was the manor again, squatting on the opposite hill. Even from this distance its malevolence seemed to reach out to me, to lay an icy finger on my cheek. So dismaying was the thought of going back that I had the urge to cry out, stop, to tell him to turn back and drive away, anywhere, just so long as we were putting distance between ourselves and Ravenswood. I didn't care where we went, and I realized suddenly that what I really wanted was to stay with James. Yes, something had happened down there in that clearing near that deserted lodge. Even in my confusion I knew with certainty that something had happened to me in those few moments from which there was no turning back. However indefinable, a watershed in my life had been reached. I wished I had it within my power just then to tell James how I felt, but as he had said, there was plenty of time. With time, I was sure, would come understanding, without the necessity for words. Words could be superfluous, and in the meantime I could still feel the warmth of his body, the strength of his arms, and the pressure of his lips against mine.

As we descended the hill, I noticed the riders returning to the manor from the hunt. With the dogs in the van, they were heading up the slope from the valley below us, their red coats vivid against the emerald green of the grass. Their coattails flying, they held themselves forward and up from the saddle as the horses' hooves pounded the turf.

"There they are," James observed. "Back from the fray with huge appetites and awfully boring anecdotes. There'll probably be deviled kidneys for breakfast. I wonder if they caught the fox."

At the bottom of the hill we turned onto the stone bridge where James had picked me up what seemed hours earlier, but in fact could not have been much more than half an hour. The riders had disappeared over the brow of the hill.

"I hope not," I said. "It all seems so unnecessary. All the dressing up and ritual. I'm with the fox all the way."

"It gives them something to do," James said. "They think it has definite social value."

The towers of the manor were above us again, slowly circling as we wound our way up the steep hill in low gear. Then we were at the top of the hill, driving along the tree-lined avenue toward the walls of the manor. The hunting party was milling around in the courtyard, dismounting from their horses and mopping their foreheads with handkerchiefs. We pulled up just inside the courtyard. The dogs had been leashed and taken away to their kennels at the rear of the mansion. The horses, their sleek flanks gleaming with perspiration, were being led away to the stables. The riders stood in groups at the foot of the steps leading up to the main entrance, smoking cigarettes and talking quietly among themselves. There seemed to be a low but sustained air of excitement. They looked across at us curiously. Many of the faces were new to me, and I guessed they were local people. Looking quite debonair, and wearing his cap at a jaunty angle, Rendal Griers was idly tapping his riding crop against one polished brown boot. Colonel Cross's face was flushed, and Geraldine Willoughby, heavy and awkward in her tight-fitting costume, talked breathlessly of the excitement of the chase. Lady Watmough, her cap sitting askew on her untidy mop of gray hair, her eyes narrowed against the sun, strode across to join us as we climbed out of the car. She didn't look pleased.

"Damn washout," she complained. "Blighter got away. Too damn cunning. Well, how about breakfast? A hearty breakfast, and then I'll show you the library." She shook her head in disgust. "Very disappointing. One stakes so much on success."

The acrid smell of horses' sweat still lingered. "Never mind, Florence," Griers called cheerfully. "The game's the thing—remember. Don't you think that's right, Miss Baker?"

"I suppose you're right," I replied unenthusiastically.

Lady Watmough swung away and clapped her hands together. "Come on, everybody. Breakfast on the table. Kill the old appetite. Let's go."

SECRET AT RAVENSWOOD

I was looking past her to the others. More specifically, I was looking for Everard. As I suspected, he wasn't there. Nor, I noticed, was the quiet American, Martin Keenan.

13

Our footsteps echoed along the narrow stone passages, and I had the strange feeling that time had become compressed and that Lady Watmough was still leading me to my room in the old wing. There were the same passages, the same doors and archways. We climbed the same steps, and our footsteps had the same hollow ring. The walls were just as black and impenetrable, and we might well have been starting all over again. I had just arrived at Ravenswood, and Lady Watmough was showing

SECRET AT RAVENSWOOD

me to my room. I could almost imagine that I would sleep soundly, with no interruption, no dragging footsteps and unearthly laughter, and in the morning could go for a walk in the surrounding countryside without the expectation of stumbling across a body. But that was wishful thinking, and the feeling soon passed. Striding energetically ahead of me, still dressed in her hunting outfit, Lady Watmough was conducting me to the library.

"No need to mention anything about this," James had said before he had left. "I'll handle everything. Just leave it to me, and carry on as normal."

"If that's possible," I had murmured unhappily.

I had been sorry to see him go, and had walked back with him to his car. He had kissed me again, and I had clung to him for some moments before I had finally let him go.

We came to the grille in the wall, and once more there was the impression of expectant stillness. I hurried past after Lady Watmough.

Breakfast had been a rowdy affair. Even if they had failed to catch the fox, everyone seemed cheerful. There was a lot of laughter, and there had been champagne with the kedgeree, kippers, and kidneys. My appetite had gone, and I picked at the food. There had still been no sign of either Everard or Martin Keenan, and I had sat deep in thought. Rendal

Griers had come across to talk to me, and although I felt I was reasonably responsive, my heart just wasn't in it. I was aware that he was exerting his considerable charm on me.

Instead of continuing along the passage where my room was situated, we turned up another flight of upward-spiraling steps. We were climbing up the tower of the old wing.

I could only assume that Everard Watmough and Martin Keenan hadn't gone on the hunt, and that either of them could have been responsible for killing Jamil. It could have been anyone, but despite James's reservations, my mind kept coming back to Everard. Even if tenuously, I was able to connect him with the car that had stopped among the trees. It had all the makings of a prearranged meeting. Everard could have been desperate enough to kill Jamil. He could have reached breaking point, particularly if Jamil had something on him, was blackmailing him in some way. Everard was heavily in debt. He needed money. He could have been desperate enough to act, as James had suggested, in a highly uncharacteristic fashion.

The steps seemed to wind endlessly above us. Daylight gleamed faintly from the walls. Martin Keenan also hadn't been with the hunt, which meant he also had an opportunity. But I knew nothing at all about him except that he was American and that he had known Sir Charles Watmough. I remembered how watch-

SECRET AT RAVENSWOOD

ful he had been during dinner the night before, and the striking impression I had had that there was nothing he missed. He had retired early, and I hadn't seen him since—as I hadn't seen Everard since. The other thing I remembered about Keenan was that although he was very quiet, he seemed to be possessed of a barely contained inner energy that in some men could be dangerous if it were not kept in proper check.

Finally we reached the top of the steps. Ahead of us was another passage, at the end of which was a heavy metal door.

There was a combination lock set in the door. I watched while Lady Watmough fiddled with it, setting the numbers into place in rapid, dazzling succession. "I've written the combination down for you," she said, reaching into her jacket pocket and handing me a folded slip of paper, "so you can come and go as you please. Don't lose it, now." The lock made a slight grating sound as it turned. Then there was a click, and she pushed the door open.

"Here we are," she said. "The lion's den."

The room was huge and semicircular. It was musty, and the shafts of sunlight that slanted down from the narrow windows set high in the outer wall of the tower were full of dust. From a landing inside the door, steps led down into the well of the library. I moved out to the edge of the landing and stared in awe at the room which was, to say the least, impressive.

From the floor to the high vaulted ceiling, the circular walls were covered with books. The shelves extended in a virtually unbroken line around the room. About halfway up the wall was a narrow iron catwalk that was reached by an iron ladder. There were so many books, stretching around me in fine array, reached by sliding ladders attached by rollers to a rod at the top of the shelves. Beneath the shelves were a desk, bare except for a green leather blotting pad and a reading lamp, an armchair, and another metal door.

"It's all here," Lady Watmough observed. "The sum of one man's folly." She made a broad sweeping gesture with one outstretched arm. "Volumes and volumes, as you can see. Extraordinary lengths he took to bag some of them. Great sacrifices. Always prowling around the most outlandish places. A lot of it hush-hush, of course. He could get away with it. Had the lingo and the style. Kept his eyes open and wrote long reports. Didn't say what for, but one could read between the lines. H.M. goverment showed its gratitude, honors and all that. It was on one of these secret missions of his that I lost my eye. I'm sure you've been wondering. Yes, up near the frontier, desolate country, spotting out the lay of the land, something to do with oil—always something to do

SECRET AT RAVENSWOOD

with oil—and these Kurdish tribesmen started taking potshots at us. Bullet ricocheted, chip of rock flew into my eye. Now you know."

Her voice reverberated around the room. Dust motes danced in the sunlight. I followed Lady Watmough as she began to move down the steps. She pointed to the metal door. "That's the safe. The manuscripts are in there." Taking a ring of keys from her pocket, she jangled it in the palm of her hand and crossed to the metal door. She took some time to select one key from the ring, muttering under her breath, her good eye squinting in concentration as she turned the keys over. Finally she selected one, and fitting it into the lock of the door, turned it and opened the door.

The safe was long and narrow, stretching back into the thick wall. Lady Watmough switched on a light, which flickered and cast a sickly yellow glow over the double row of filing cabinets. Above the cabinets were a number of pigeonholes filled with thin metal cylinders. Lady Watmough nodded to them.

"The manuscripts. The cylinders are marked. They'll tell you which one is which." She backed out of the safe. "All right, now. I'll leave you to it. Rummage to your heart's content. Make sure the safe's locked when you're finished. Just pull the door to. Same with the outside door. Take your time." She wrinkled her face in disgust. "Ugh, this air is so stale and musty. Give me a whiff of clean fresh air any time."

She moved across the room to the steps. "I hope Everard's all right," I called after her. "I didn't see him this morning, and I was wondering if he was all right."

"He comes and goes," she said without looking back. "No one knows where he is half the time." She climbed the steps to the landing and disappeared through the doorway.

I listened to her footsteps receding along the passage until I could hear them no more, then sighed. I had my work cut out for me, and I didn't know where to start. I looked at the rows of metal cylinders. The one item in the collection that was uppermost in my mind was, naturally, the Bokhara Commentary. I began to pull out the metal cylinders. The names of the manuscripts they contained had been typed on small labels that had been stuck to the end of each cylinder. Most of the names were unfamiliar to me. I replaced each cylinder as I took it out and saw it was not the one I was seeking. There would be time later to compare them with the inventory, which was still in my room. This exercise was purely one of familiarization.

I found the Bokhara Commentary sitting alone in one of the pigeonholes. I took it out of the safe to the desk and switched on the lamp. Then, sitting down at the desk, I screwed the lid from the end of the cylinder, which I up-

SECRET AT RAVENSWOOD

ended over the blotting pad and carefully eased out its contents.

The Bokhara Commentary. Here it was at last, fabled, legendary, and probably a hoax. The parchment was thin and fragile, discolored with age, as I slowly opened it out, holding it at the edges so that it wouldn't roll back again. I stared down at the elegant Arabic script, not understanding what it meant, but letting my eyes run down the neat tracery, the rows and rows of intricate lettering, and somehow their magic became absorbed in me. I allowed my mind to wander, the script became blurred, and I could see the rolling sand dunes scored and striated by the driving desert winds, the plodding camel trains, towns with their walls and buildings glaring white in the merciless heat, the crowded bazaars and the long caravans laden with spices and silks noisily preparing to set out on the Golden Road, the domes and minarets that reflected the blue of the sky. I could almost hear the cry of the muezzin calling the faithful to prayer, the hubbub in the marketplace. It was so far away in time and place. I released the edges of the script and let it fall back into a roll.

Rising from the chair, I stared up at the tiers of books that ranged above me in a circle, so that I had the feeling that I was standing at the bottom of an enormous cylinder. I turned my head this way and that, viewing the books from differing perspectives. They seemed to move with the movement of my head, circling slowly above me, massive volumes, a treasury of Islamic thought and wisdom, the great poets and philosophers in soft leather bindings. Here was contained an enormous wealth of knowledge. I began to turn slowly in the middle of the floor, staring up at the books, allowing myself to get an initial feel of them. The detailed work would come later. The light from the open safe spilled out onto the floor. Shadows gathered thickly in the corners of the room, hardly touched by the slanting shafts of dusty light.

I thought I heard a sound behind me. I swung to face the landing and the open outer door. But all I saw were shadows, and I guessed I must have been mistaken.

Suddenly I had the unnerving feeling that I was not alone in the room, that there was a presence close to me, watching me. I peered even more intently into the shadows, and although I still saw nothing, the feeling persisted. Then I heard another sound, this time from somewhere above me. Craning my head, I anxiously scanned the towering bookshelves and the narrow catwalk that ringed the room.

Abruptly, and with a sick jolting sensation, I noticed a movement on the catwalk, a gradual shifting of the shadows, which fell back as a tall dark figure materialized in the gloom behind the shafts of gray light. I stared up at it, transfixed, my feet seemingly rooted to the spot. I blinked, and blinked again as the outline of the figure slowly became more distinct. It was a figure in a long dark cloak, with a white ruff at the neck. The face was in shadow. .

Then there was the sound of soft laughter, which gradually increased in volume—deep, rolling, and reverberating, deflected from the many hundreds of books that surrounded me. It came down to me in waves. The figure began to move forward into the light. I took a step back and came up against the side of the desk. I edged sideways. The evil laughter was steadily building up to a bloodcurdling crescendo.

Now, as the figure came out to the catwalk railing, I could make out the face, pale and punched with shadow, but with the long nose, the shoulder-length hair and forked beard, unmistakably that of the Black Baron himself, Sir Mondrath Watmough, who had been dead for at least five hundred years.

As he reached for the ladder, and with his cloak flying began to descend it with the agility of a monkey, I choked back a startled sob and began to run across the room to the steps. I could hear him behind me, a soft thud as he jumped from the ladder onto the floor, then the padding of his running feet as he chased me, gained on me. I reached the steps, and was scrambling up them as fast as I could, when I slipped and grazed my knee on the sharp edge of one step. I was dragging myself up onto my feet, my fingers clawing the cold, pitted stone, when I felt iron fingers digging cruelly into my shoulder, wrenching me sharply back, and I was falling, flying through the air briefly, until something struck the back of my head. There was a loud clanging sound, which quickly faded, and then everything went black.

14

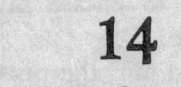

There was a slow rocking movement, and I felt extremely cold. Then the motion ceased, but the cold remained. There was a searing pain at the back of my head, and I huddled myself into a ball to try to force it away. My hand reached out, and when it touched something that felt like ice, instantly recoiled. With the vague sense of motion, pushing down through the sharp, billowing waves of pain, had come the crazy sensation that I was riding on the back of a camel, plodding across a desert, and in the distance the rays of the sun glanced from the minarets of the distant town with such blinding force that they hurt my eyes. But there was no heat in the sun. I had never felt so cold. The white light pulsed, became concentrated and as sharp as a lance driven in behind my eyes. I moaned, and the sound came from far away. The pain ebbed and flowed with thunderous intensity, carrying me forward with its thrust, then dragging me back. The light sharpened even more until it was just an icily blazing pinpoint that jabbed through my closed eyelids. I hugged myself tightly in an attempt to keep warm, but the cold had eaten right through my clothing and flesh to encase my bones in a coating of brittle ice.

I fought the cold and the pulsing pain. My eyes were squeezed shut. I fought the slow, inevitable return of consciousness. Gradually it came back to me, in fragments at first, then gathering form and substance until a shadowy picture was partly complete.

Shadows—there had been the shadows all around me, more consolidated than dispersed by the weak light. The books stretching almost up to the ceiling, and the feeling that I was standing at one end of a huge cylinder. Then, on the catwalk, a figure materializing out of the shadows, a tall figure in a cloak, with a forked beard, shoulder-length black hair, and a long nose. And then, as the fiendish laughter had begun to roll around me, I had tried to get out of the room. There had been the fleeting impression of the figure scrambling agilely down the iron ladder. I had stumbled on the steps, a hand had grabbed my shoulder, and then I was falling. . . .

I lay still for a long time, hugging myself and hardly daring to move as full consciousness made its slow, insidious progress. My legs and arms were cramped. My fingers were numb, and I moved them to restore the feeling in them. I could faintly hear the sound of dripping water. The Black Baron—it was impossible. It couldn't be possible. But I had seen the portrait in the hall downstairs, and it was the same man who had sprung down the ladder after me. I could still hear the laughter that had drummed into me from all sides of the room. Slowly I opened my eyes, preparing myself for a renewed onslaught of pain, but thankfully there wasn't much pain. I lifted one hand and gingerly touched the lump at the back of my head, which felt to be about the size of a duck's egg. The skin around it was very tender, and as I gently probed, needles of pain darted from the point of contact. My head throbbed, but the pain was slowly losing its white-hot intensity. Carefully bringing myself up into a sitting position, and fighting back the waves of nausea that were triggered by the movement, I looked around me, allowing my eyes to become accustomed to the darkness.

I was in a chamber or an alcove of some sort. There was a wall behind me, and a shallow flight of steps in front of me. My eyes strained into the darkness at the foot of the steps and could just make out the wall of a passage that led away into the darkness. The dripping sound came from that direction. The penetrating cold was numbing my body, and I had no idea how long I had been unconscious.

He must have carried me here from the library, and dumped me on the cold stone floor, probably meaning to come back at a later time. I was in great danger, and it was obvious I couldn't stay here. I didn't know where I was, although I suspected I was somewhere in the old dungeons of the manor, and I had to try to find my way out before the Black Baron returned—*if* he meant to return. It was the uncertainty of what he intended that was the most racking. I listened, but all I could hear was the steady dripping of water in the distance . .

Supporting myself against the wall behind me, I slowly hauled myself to my feet. My head spun, and there was a richly nauseous sensation in my stomach, and as I steadied myself against the wall, I thought I was about to faint. Then the dizziness and the nausea passed, and I felt a little better. My head was still throbbing sharply.

Unsteadily, and supporting myself against the wall, I made my way down the steps. I took them slowly, one at a time, stopping on each one to listen and stare into the darkness ahead. There was light coming from somewhere, but it was very faint. Still with my hand on the wall, as much to guide me now as support me, I moved along the passage. The air was stale and gritty, and my whole being was as taut and ready to snap as a very fine watch spring.

There was a break in the wall, and another passage opened to my left. I stopped, undecided which way to go. I had the unpleasant feeling that it didn't matter which way I turned, the result would be the same and I would find no way out of my prison. There would be more passages, and each one, I was sure, would bring me closer to the center of the maze. I decided at last to continue along the passage I was already on, where the light seemed to be a little stronger. With every step I took, I expected to hear the crazed laughter of the man in the cloak who had brought me here. Perhaps he was watching me now, playing some sort of cat-and-mouse game with me, allowing me to go so far before, with a hitch of his cloak and a flash of his teeth, he pounced on me. The ghost was playing games, filling in time, alleviating the boredom of being a ghost confined within the grim gray walls of Ravenswood Manor. I hastily admonished myself. My mind was straying. I was being fanciful, when all my effort should have been concentrated on getting myself out of the place, or trying at least to summon help. I could disappear from the face of the earth and no one would know where to look for me. Except Sir Mondrath Watmough, who was only a ghost anyway.

A ghost. . . . I didn't believe in ghosts. I never had believed in ghosts. I had felt those strong fingers digging into my shoulder and dragging me back. They hadn't been the fingers of a ghost. They had been very real, and had belonged to somebody who was masquerading as the manor's original incumbent, who had known the family legend and decided to exploit it. The same person whose footsteps had dragged outside my door, who had tried to enter my room, and whose laughter had followed his retreat along the passage.

The passage broadened, and the light became fractionally stronger. Suddenly, from just in front of me, there was a leathery flapping sound, and as I recoiled in horror against the wall, my heart lurched up near my throat, I saw something winging rapidly away into the diffused darkness ahead of me. With my back against the wall, I waited for the flurry within me to subside before going on, my senses even more alert, if that was possible, and prepared, I hoped, for similar shocks.

I came to the end of the passage, and in front

SECRET AT RAVENSWOOD

of me was a large empty chamber. At the far end of the chamber, a steep flight of steps rose to a grilled gate, the bars of which were silhouetted grimly by the indistinct gray light that filtered down from behind it. Other passages opened from the chamber. I crossed quickly to the steps, and was about to start climbing them to the gate when I noticed something wedged in the corner between the steps and the wall, an indistinguishable lumpy shape in the darkness.

Moving away from the steps, I approached the bundle in the corner. My breathing was shallow and my heart was beating faster again as I bent forward over the bundle, trying to make out what it could be. Then, when I did recognize it for what it was, I gasped and stepped hurriedly back. Yet I was unable to take my eyes from Everard's upturned face and the staring eyes that saw nothing, nor would see anything ever again.

15

I stopped backing away, and stood motionless, staring down at Everard's crumpled body, which I could see more clearly now in the dim light from the gate above me. His body was twisted grotesquely, his head lolling at an angle that suggested his neck had been broken. His legs were doubled up beneath him. He looked rather like a broken doll in a mauve sweater and beige twill trousers. As the shock of the discovery began to wear off, it was hard to believe, in this light, that he had even been real.

SECRET AT RAVENSWOOD

I didn't know what to think. I guess, at the back of my mind, in the time since I had regained consciousness and tried to fathom the puzzle of the Black Baron, I had believed it to be Everard all the time. There was a resemblance between him and Sir Mondrath, and if, for reasons best known to himself, he had decided to disguise himself as his distant ancestor, he could make a reasonable job of it, assisted by the shadows and the fear induced by that terrible laughter. I hadn't actually let the thought protrude into my consciousness, to cement itself into a definite suspicion, but it had been there, the thought, the germ of the thought. But now Everard was dead, and I knew I had to rethink the matter. I glanced up at the gate. I was wasting time in idle speculation. It was still dangerous for me to be here. It was dangerous for me to remain in the manor. How I wished I had gone with James. He had told me I needn't come back to the manor, and he was so right. But it was too late to think about that now.

I was staring back down at Everard, when suddenly I was aware that the darkness had intensified. Fear grabbed me as I spun and looked up at the gate. When I saw him standing there behind the gate, I gave a sharp cry of alarm and backed rapidly away. Sir Mondrath had returned. Now he was brandishing a sword.

"Aha, my pretty one," he cried hoarsely, pushing open the gate, which swung reluctantly against his pressure, and leaping through the opening onto the landing. "I am coming for you."

The light was behind him, and I couldn't see his face. He stood there at the top of the steps, his booted feet well apart, his cloak draped from his shoulders and his hands on his hips. He tossed his head, and the faint light caught his thick, ropy black hair.

"A fine wench to quench a man's thirst," he said, and laughed. "All these years I have been waiting for one as comely as you. The wait was worthwhile, methinks."

It was so silly. It was pure ham, and I think it was that that frightened me even more. It certainly startled me. I was still backing away from the foot of the steps, while he stood above me in the brash pose of a medieval swashbuckler. Although I couldn't see his teeth, I knew he was grinning at me. I asked myself if I was really seeing him or if he was the figment of a strained, overworked imagination. As I backed away, I looked wildly around for a way to escape this antiquated madman. All around me, passages opened from the chamber. I could take any one of them without knowing where it would lead me. I didn't even know which was the passage that had brought me to the chamber.

I was caught in a flurry of indecision. The Black Baron had moved right to the top of the

SECRET AT RAVENSWOOD

steps. Behind him, the gate was half-open. Suddenly, with an ear-splitting whoop, with a sweeping flourish of his sword, and with his cloak streaming behind him, he leaped from the top of the steps onto the floor, came down heavily on his feet, lurched, staggered, and muttered, "Damn!" I didn't wait. I sprinted toward the nearest passage.

I ran and ran, into the darkness, unable to see where I was going. At times, I cannoned into the wall, and pushed myself away from it. I could hear the Baron lumbering along behind me.

"Come back, my pretty," he yelled. "You can't hide from me. I shall find you, no matter where you go." Then he yelped and muttered, "Blasted ankle!" There was a quick fluttering through the air in front of me, then another. The passage seemed to curve. Behind me, the Black Baron was still calling me to come back.

I was feeling my way along the wall. Then there was no wall, but an opening of some sort. Carefully feeling my way, I moved into the opening, finding the wall again and following it to an angle where it met another wall. I ran my hand along that wall until I reached another right angle. I was in an alcove or a cell. Pressing myself into the angle, I held my breath, waited, and prayed my pursuer didn't have a flashlight with him, not the sort of equipment normally carried by a family ghost.

I began to shiver violently, and tightly clenched my jaw muscles so he wouldn't hear the clacking of my teeth.

I heard him coming along the passage, and the clang of his sword as it struck the stone wall. "Ho, ho, ho," he cried with halfhearted jubilation. "I'm coming to get you. You can't get away from me now."

I was holding my breath until a pain developed in my chest. There was an ache in my jaw from the effort to keep my teeth from chattering. I pushed myself as far as I could into the angle of the wall, but still felt I was exposed, that he couldn't help but see me there.

Making a great deal of noise for a ghost, he came running heavily past my hiding place. From where I was standing I could vaguely make him out as he charged past the cell. Fighting back the urge to run the moment he had passed the entrance, I waited until his footsteps had receded along the passage, then, letting go my contained breath with a soft gasp, pushed myself away from the wall to the passage. I could hear Sir Mondrath blundering along it in the opposite direction from which I began to run. At any moment now he would realize I was no longer in front of him, and would turn back. I sprinted along the passage to the central chamber and the steps that led up to the open gate.

I had come farther than I thought I had.

SECRET AT RAVENSWOOD

There seemed to be no end to the passage, and I was beginning to wonder if I hadn't turned the wrong way and that I was just about to crash heavily into the Black Baron on his way back. It was a chilling thought, but I kept running, silently praying that I was heading in the right direction after all. Then I perceived the dim diffusion of light in front of me, the end of the passage, and the chamber beyond.

I rushed out into the chamber, cutting diagonally across it from the passage to the steps. I could see Everard's huddled, twisted body beneath them, once more a black, indistinguishable, untidy shape in the light-splintered darkness. I couldn't hear any sound from the passage behind me. The Black Baron must surely have realized by now that I had managed to elude him. I ran up the slippery stone steps to the gate, and without looking back into the cavernous, shadowy chamber beneath me, slipped through the open doorway.

I was in another passage. To my right, steps led upward. I knew where I was. The gate was the same one that had given me strange vibrations every time I passed it. Not thinking, I sprinted up the steps. I was halfway when I realized I should have gone the other way, back toward the main part of the manor, where there would be people, where, for a while, I would be safe—if I managed to reach it. But it was too late to turn back. I could hear sounds behind me again. I had to keep going.

I came to the passage that led to my room, and for a moment I hesitated. If I could reach my room and lock the door, I might gain a temporary respite, but I couldn't stay there forever. I would have to come out sometime, and I couldn't be sure of knowing that he wouldn't be waiting for me. I was trapped. I could hear his footsteps drawing closer. He had reached the bottom of the steps, and was climbing them after me. Next to me, the spiral steps led up to the library. Still without thinking, still caught in an unreasoning panic, I dragged myself up the steps, gasping for breath as my feet carried me upward, seemingly of their own volition. The library. I had nowhere else to go. If I could reach the library and slam the door shut behind me, so that he couldn't get in . . . Another respite, and I would be in an even worse position than I would have been if I had locked myself in my room. I should have turned the other way when I came through the gate. There I had a chance. Now I had no chance at all. I followed the curve of the steps, pushing myself from one wall to the next. I would never make it. I could hear him close behind me, gaining on me.

Finally I reached the passage, with the library door open at the end of it. A few more yards, an extra effort. My head was throbbing

SECRET AT RAVENSWOOD

fiercely, my vision blurred. The library door was so close to me, yet so far away. My body felt so heavy as I lurched toward the door. The Black Baron was just behind me. The library door. I virtually flung myself at it. The Black Baron had reached the passage. As I pushed myself against the door, I glanced fearfully over my shoulder. He was closer than I had thought, only a few feet away, thundering along the passage behind me, a frightening picture of bloodthirstiness and medieval retribution as he made quick sweeping and jabbing motions with his sword. The shadows darkened his face, and his lips were drawn back over strong white teeth. His cloak flapped wildly around him as he ran.

I moved quickly into the library, then, grabbing the door, tried to push it shut against him. But then, as I was closing it, he flung all his weight against it, much too powerfully for me to be able to withstand it. The force sent me staggering back across the landing as the Black Baron leaped gleefully into the room after me. I was trapped. There was nowhere I could go.

16

Holding the sword out before him, he advanced across the landing toward me. I backed away from him to the steps that led down into the room. His face was still in shadow, but I could see that it was covered with what looked like thick white greasepaint. The heavy shoulder-length hair was obviously false, as was the long Watmough nose. The dark eyes glinted wickedly, and his smile was dazzling. I recognized it immediately.

"Well, you certainly led me a merry chase,"

SECRET AT RAVENSWOOD

he said softly, calmly, in a very familiar voice. "But now I've caught you at last. You didn't really think you could get away, did you?"

I was still trying to catch my breath. I had reached the top of the steps. "Why?" I gasped.

The sword was pointing at my throat. He was still coming toward me. He laughed, and with his other hand gestured toward the costume he was wearing. "Why this? I guess it's the ham in me. A little fun while I work. A little style. A sense of the dramatic. And this is such an old mansion." He chuckled. He really was performing like a very bad actor of the old school. "I always did have aspirations to the stage. Did a spot of it once, amateur productions, musicals, and somehow it got into the blood. I've been quite enjoying myself, and I meant to frighten you out of your wits last night. You locked your door. I wasn't sure if you would or not. The costume came with me in my bag. Thought it'd be fun to dress up like old Sir Mondrath and wander restlessly about the old manor for a while. Get the feel of the place."

I was backing down the steps. With the sword still pointed at my throat, he followed me. "It was you who killed Jamil, and Everard," I said, stalling for time. I didn't know what he intended doing with me, but I wanted to put it off for as long as possible.

The shadows played across his white-painted face. The forks of his beard were rigid. "Quite a wag, the old Sir Mondrath—what? A lusty fellow indeed." He was still smiling. "Yes, I did kill them. They were in the way, and now it's your turn. An accident, I think." He looked over my head at the book-lined walls and the catwalk. "A fall. It could be nasty, but quick. The most natural thing in the world. You were reaching up for something, and you slipped." We moved slowly down the steps. "Yes, they were in my way, poor chaps, and I had to get rid of them. Everard first, then the other one. Had to break away from the hunt to do it, a small risk, so long as it didn't take too long, and no one missed me. Even so, I could have told 'em I got lost or something, decided to take a shortcut, no real problem. I saw you coming, and waited until you found the body. You started running. Frightened out of your wits, you were. Running through the autumn leaves, a sylphlike figure in the forest. The body, the corpse, the cadaver, the erstwhile. Had to move fast. Extra time needed. Dispose of the dear departed. Got it as far as the disused quarry, and chances are no one will find it for some time to come. Had to walk back to where I left the horse, through brambles, mud, not exceptionally pleasant, I might tell you. And Everard—waspish, languid Everard. No one will find him in the cellar. No one ever goes down there."

We were at the bottom of the steps. The safe was still open, the light still on, and I saw

SECRET AT RAVENSWOOD

that the drawers of the filing cabinet had been pulled open and that there were papers scattered everywhere. I glanced across at the desk. The Bokhara Commentary had gone.

The phony Black Baron gestured with his sword. "The ladder. Start climbing."

The iron ladder reached up to the catwalk high above me. I hesitated. I had to keep him talking. "Why did you have to kill them?"

His smile seemed to have developed into a fixture. "I told you, my sweet. They were in my way. We were all after the same thing. I had to eliminate the competition."

"The Bokhara Commentary," I hazarded.

He nodded. "Spot on. Congrats are due. The commentary, and other material that might be useful when rainy days beckon. So much hinges on that piece of paper. It's worth a fortune. It must be, or else they wouldn't be offering so much."

"Who are 'they'?"

"A faction. Can one ever lose sight of them? There really is a power struggle going on in that poor benighted desert country. One lot against the other, spearheading to power. I don't know. I don't care. I was made an offer too good to refuse, and I was warned about the darling opposition. Do you really see me as a killer? Do I not have sparkling, disingenuous eyes?"

"I don't . . ."

"Everard and his friend were working for

that splendid opposition. One has to be sporting, you know. Salute the enemy. Cut their throats, and salute them. Honor the dead. And none of us could do anything until you came to open up the safe. Lady Watmough, actually, but she's a tough old stick. A fiend and a dragon—*la formidable*. Wild horses could drag nothing from her, and no one dare try. So subtle, subtle is the game. Play the fish." His voice sharpened a little. "Now, are you going to climb that ladder, or am I to run you through on the spot and take you to join Everard in the cellar?" He gestured again with the sword to underscore the threat. "Do state."

I took hold of the iron supports and placed one foot on the bottommost rung. He stood behind me. The catwalk looked to be an enormous distance above me. I began to climb the ladder, hauling myself up past the rows of old and dusty books. It was a long, slow climb. I could hear him on the ladder behind me, and glanced back down at him. As he climbed, the sword clanged against the railing. I had thought briefly that if he were close enough behind me, I might be able to kick back at him, catch him off his guard, a risky maneuver that might just cause him to lose his balance, but he was too far behind me to enable me to achieve any sort of surprise. I continued to climb hand over hand, putting distance between myself and the floor.

Finally I pulled myself up onto the catwalk.

"Stand back now," the Black Baron ordered. "Right back."

It was an opportunity to get him as he drew himself up onto the platform, but he had apparently anticipated that something of the sort had crossed my mind. He was holding the sword above his head, free of the railing, jabbing it toward me. A stray beam of sunlight caught the side of his thickly painted face. The wig and beard were made of horsehair. He scrambled up onto the catwalk next to me.

"Frankly, I didn't expect you to come around so soon," he said, smiling crookedly at me. "I was going to come back after I had obtained what I came here to get, and finish off the job at leisure. But . . ." He spread his hands, and for the first time a note of wistfulness crept into his voice. "It really is too bad, you know. You're a very attractive girl. So fair . . . so *shining*, really. And young, life ahead of you, great opportunities. A pity, but necessary." He brought the sword up again and pointed it at me. The double-edged blade looked very sharp.

There was nowhere for me to run. He was standing between me and the ladder. He shifted to one side, away from the top of the ladder, and made a quick jabbing motion with the sword. "Either way, it will be messy. I suggest you jump. It will look more like an accident."

I looked into his eyes, but they were dark

and completely devoid of life. I pushed myself back against the rows of books. He gestured again, impatiently, and brought the sword up so that the point of it was only inches from my throat. He took a step forward, and the point came even closer. "If you won't jump . . ." Suddenly his free hand darted forward too quickly for me to get out of the way, and grabbed my arm, his strong fingers digging into my flesh. He jerked me roughly forward. I tried to twist free of his grasp, but he was too strong. He swung me, and pressed me back against the catwalk railing, dragging me along it to the opening at the point where the ladder reached the platform. My feet slipped on the iron surface. He was breathing heavily through his nose. I gripped the railing and hung on to it grimly. He swore, and brought the flat of the sword hard down against my knuckles. The blow hurt, but I still gripped the railing. He struck again, at the same time pulling me toward the opening. He struck my hand a third time with the sword, and this time the skin broke. A drop of blood welled and elongated, and my grip loosened involuntarily. He tugged me forward, and my hand fell away from the railing. He dropped the sword, and grasping me with his other hand, whirled me to the opening in front of him.

There was nothing beneath me. The stone floor was a long way down, and the rows and rows of books swam before my eyes. They heaved and lurched as the Baron, his eyes still cold and lifeless, like fathomless holes set in the thickly caked makeup, forced me back over the edge of the catwalk. My feet scuffled on the iron platform.

Then something happened, I heard a shout from below and saw that the Black Baron's eyes were staring past me with an expression of flickering surprise. His hold on me relaxed sufficiently to enable me to break free and swing to one side. He made a move as if to forestall me, but it lacked real compunction. There was another shout from below.

"Hold it right there, sweetheart," a voice called. "Don't make another move."

I stared gratefully down at Martin Keenan, who was standing on the landing just inside the door, and at the revolver he was pointing unerringly up at the Black Baron. Then I saw James just behind him, and knew that everything was going to be all right.

"Oh . . . balls," Rendal Griers said, taking off his false nose.

17

"You mean you knew all along that something like this would happen?" I was more than a little annoyed; I had come very close to being killed. Two men had already been killed, and Martin Keenan was looking positively smug.

"A suspicion—nothing more than that." He was puffing thoughtfully on his pipe and staring past me at the green landscape that rolled away from the foot of the hill. "A man of many parts, and most of them shady. A manipulator,

SECRET AT RAVENSWOOD

a commodities man, a broker. We had him checked out, and it seemed to us he was a likely candidate."

The excitement was over. The police had come and gone, and Rendal Griers, still in his costume, his face covered with greasepaint, had been taken away. Now that I had recovered from my experience in the library, my annoyance had had time to develop, and it was directed more particularly at James.

"You mean you *knew* something like this would happen?"

At least he had the grace to look shamefaced about it. "We guessed something would happen, but weren't sure what. When Mr. Keenan here approached our office and suggested I could keep an eye on you while he took a look around . . . Anyway, it's over now. No great harm done."

"But there very nearly was," I wailed. "I was almost killed back there, and if you hadn't come when you did, a second later . . ." The words dried up. Even now, the prospect of what nearly happened was too awful to contemplate.

Martin Keenan glanced at his wristwatch. He looked like a man in a hurry. "The important thing is that we have the Bokhara Commentary," he said. "And the opposition has been flushed. As long as I can get it back in one piece. It could still be risky, but it's a risk well worth taking."

163

"I don't understand it at all," I said, looking from one of them to the other. Pale blue smoke drifted up from the bowl of Keenan's pipe. "*Why* is the Commentary so important?"

"Ah." Keenan drew on his pipe. "The Commentary itself—no, that's a forgery. Dead issue, long gone. No, it's what's on the *back* of the document that's so important. Without going into too much detail, there's a plan drawn up by Sir Charles Watmough during one of his explorations outside Sirashar—explorations that had a specific purpose, which was to map out new oil deposits. In the border country, very wild and barren, he found evidence of important oil deposits. Massive. He drew up the plan, and transferred it to the back of the Commentary, which had only recently come into his possession. It was a well-guarded secret which he shared with only a handful of others, including Jules Barthelmy, powerful men who agreed—conspired, if you like—to keep it a secret, surely anticipating the time when there would be a shortage of oil such as we are experiencing today. And now the time is ripe to utilize that knowledge, exploit it, especially with the revolution raging in that country at the present time. A little juggling, if you like, but it's necessary to ensure that that part of the country at least doesn't fall into . . . unsympathetic hands. A question of strategic and tactical skills, but there are experts for that sort of thing."

"But if the oil has been there all the time," I said, "why didn't anybody else find it?"

"Those things can be arranged, as long as there's money. Even tribesmen can be supplied with money and weapons to stage their interminable warfare, to ward off strangers." He paused and drew again on his pipe. James was smiling at me, and I found I wasn't angry with him anymore. "The government—our government—came to hear of it . . . oh, some time back," Keenan went on. "As long as the government in Sirashar was stable, there was no need to worry. But with Iran, and everything else happening in that part of the world, we felt it was time to act, to ensure the document's safety. Unfortunately, there was a leak at the Barthelmy Institute, and the two rival contenders for power in Sirashar came to hear of the Commentary. They both tried to intercept it. There was that man Khamal who talked to you in London—oh, yes, we know about that; we've been keeping an eye on you since you came to England. He had already made an approach to your chief librarian, Milly Fellowes, who reported it to her superior at the Institute. This superior made the mistake of telling her to keep quiet about it. She threatened to take it up at a higher level. She didn't have a chance to do that, however. There was the accident—and

I would say beyond a shadow of a doubt that that was carefully stage-managed to keep her quiet. But she did leave behind the draft of a written report, which was overlooked by those responsible for the . . . accident."

The manor was behind us, and the sun was moving gradually down behind the western hills. It was very quiet. "You mean to say there is someone at the Institute who is working for those people?" I asked. "Khamal and the others?"

"There *was* someone," he corrected her. In the daylight, his eyes didn't look to be as clear as they had seemed the night before. "The matter has been handled. I can tell you this, I guess, which might help put the matter into some perspective. It was Sam Warren. He has been, as they say, rendered inoperative."

I looked at him helplessly. "Sam? Why?"

"Playing the double game. Supplying the information to anyone who was willing to pay for it."

"The way Khamal was talking," I said, "he made me believe it was the Commentary itself that was so important. Its religious significance."

"No doubt," Keenan said with a nod. "He wasn't going to tip his hand."

"And what happens now?" I asked.

"What happens?" Keenan shrugged. "I have to go now. I have to drive back to London."

SECRET AT RAVENSWOOD

"Griers took Jamil's body away," I told him. "He said something about a disused quarry."

Keenan was beginning to look a little impatient. His pipe had gone out. "Yes, yes, I know. James here—he told me what you told him. It's a matter now for the British police. They'll find him soon enough. I underestimated Griers. I was keeping an eye on him, but I didn't think he would act so soon, and so efficiently. I slipped up there. I didn't go on the hunt. I thought Griers was safely occupied for the time being, and my mind wasn't on murder. I was looking for Everard, and when I didn't find him . . . well I, had a hunch. When I came back, and learned you were in the library . . ." He shook his head. "Not a moment too soon, as they say in the classics. Griers was such a grandstander. He did have to dress up and play the fool. He took quite a lot of other material. Thought it would stand him in good stead in the future. Always the opportunist, and a very bad actor."

He began to move away from us toward the entrance. "I was nearly killed," I called after him.

He stopped and looked back at us. His eyes studied me quizzically. "Yes, perhaps you were," he said quietly. "A risk. It wasn't intended that way."

"Who are you?" I asked.

"A man in a hurry." He turned away and began walking toward the courtyard of the manor. I looked at James. He took my hand.

"Is he with the State Department? The CIA. What?"

"I'm not sure myself," James said. "You can take your pick. Does it matter? I'm in love with you. You did very well."

"Without my knowing it."

"You flushed out the demons."

"That doesn't thrill me at all."

"There's still the collection to be cataloged and shipped."

"Nor that."

"I'll be here. Lady Watmough has invited me to stay, and I'm due for some leave. I'll watch over you like a fierce guardian angel. I'll protect you from the real Black Baron." He squeezed my hand. "Let's go for a walk and watch the sunset."

We began to walk down the hill. "Tell me," I said, "are you a Berkshire Montague or a Bedford Montague?"

"I'm a Highgate Hill Montague. I went to an atrocious school."

"I do like the English."

"And me, too, I hope. I promise to make you very happy."

I gazed at him fondly. "Yes, I think you would."

Behind us, a car started. The Bokhara Commentary was on its way to America, and I didn't

SECRET AT RAVENSWOOD

care if it got there or not. It was my first weekend in England, and I hoped there weren't going to be any others like it. But I was in love, and that was all that mattered.

More Gothics from SIGNET

- [ ] **SIGNET DOUBLE GOTHIC—CURSE OF THE ISLAND POOL by Virginia Coffman and THE HIGH TERRACE by Virginia Coffman.** (#J9126—$1.95)*

- [ ] **LEGACY OF FEAR by Virginia Coffman.** (#E8860—$1.75)*

- [ ] **THE CLIFFS OF DREAD by Virginia Coffman.** (#E8301—$1.75)*

- [ ] **THE EVIL AT QUEEN'S PRIORY by Virginia Coffman.** (#E8403—$1.75)*

- [ ] **MIST AT DARKNESS by Virginia Coffman.** (#Q6138—95¢)

- [ ] **A HAUNTED PLACE by Virginia Coffman.** (#W7934—$1.50)

- [ ] **ISLE OF THE UNDEAD by Virginia Coffman.** (#W8032—$1.50)

- [ ] **VALLEY OF SHADOWS by Dorothy Daniels.** (#E9030—$1.75)*

- [ ] **THE CORMAC LEGEND by Dorothy Daniels.** (#J8655—$1.95)*

- [ ] **THE CURSE OF THE CONCULLENS by Florence Stevenson.** (#W7228—$1.50)

- [ ] **A SHADOW ON THE HOUSE by Florence Stevenson.** (#Y6520—$1.25)

- [ ] **THE LANDSEND TERROR by Julia Trevelyan.** (#E8526—$1.75)*

- [ ] **GREYTHORNE by Julia Trevelyan.** (#W7802—$1.50)

- [ ] **THE TOWER ROOM by Julia Trevelyan.** (#E8711—$1.75)*

* Price slightly higher in Canada

Buy them at your local bookstore or use this convenient coupon for ordering.

THE NEW AMERICAN LIBRARY, INC.,
P.O. Box 999, Bergenfield, New Jersey 07621

Please send me the SIGNET BOOKS I have checked above. I am enclosing $_____ (please add 50¢ to this order to cover postage and handling). Send check or money order—no cash or C.O.D.'s. Prices and numbers are subject to change without notice.

Name _____

Address _____

City _____ State _____ Zip Code _____

Allow 4-6 weeks for delivery.
This offer is subject to withdrawal without notice.